The Spanish Billionaire's Hired Bride

Rachel Lyndhurst

Entangled Publishing, LLC
2614 South Timberline Road
Suite 109
Fort Collins, CO 80525
Visit our website at www.entangledpublishing.com.

Edited by Alethea Spiridon Hopson
Cover design by Libby Murphy

ISBN   978-1-62266-85-40

Manufactured in the United States of America

First Edition October 2012

This book is dedicated to my editor, Alethea Spiridon Hopson, and publisher, Liz Pelletier. You're both amazing. Thanks for taking a chance on me.

Chapter One

"Stop right there or I'll snap your neck."

Ricardo Almanza heard the blonde's breath catch as his hand closed around her throat and pulled her backwards against his body. Her pulse was rapid beneath his fingertips, and her short gasps indicated fear. He loosened his hold. She might be a thief, but she was still a slightly-built woman and he had no intention of deliberately hurting her.

He grabbed her wrist and shook it roughly until she dropped the diamond necklace she was holding onto the bedspread. Her other hand flew to protect her throat, and she arched her back as if she was trying to look at him, or spit in his face, perhaps. Her voice was laced with panic.

"The Condesa—"

A pause. Her accent betrayed her, clearly not Catalan or a native of Ibiza and her Balearic sister islands. "Be quiet," he growled in English. "And do as I tell you."

Ricardo maneuvered her toward the edge of the bed, pushing his knees into the back of hers until her legs buckled, and she fell forward. Her face twisted against the silk coverlet and he sensed she was looking for a means of escape.

Grabbing her by the shoulders, he quickly tipped her onto her back and was suddenly staring into the widest, greenest eyes he had ever seen. They flashed like emeralds, and shallow, rapid breaths escaped her parted lips. His gaze slipped lower, snagged for a fraction of a second by the sight of her breasts as they rose and fell beneath a close-fitting black T-shirt. She reminded him of a trapped panther, beautiful, wild and poised, ready to fight back. A savage creature that would scratch his eyes out given half a chance.

He let go of his quarry and stepped backward to get a better look. The terrified blonde lay there panting, her eyes darting back and forth with terror. But a few more seconds were enough to confirm his very first thought. If he really had to take a wife someday, this was exactly how he'd want her to look.

"You should have done more research before you targeted this place." He trickled the necklace through his fingers as her eyes lasered into his. "These diamonds will never find a buyer on the black market. They're unique and each one traceable. No criminal on Ibiza worth his salt would touch them. Unless, of course, you're stealing to order."

"I'm not stealing anything," she hissed and pushed herself up onto her elbows. "I was just—"

"Just passing?" Ricardo injected a deliberately unpleasant tone into his voice, irked by the way her T-shirt now strained across her chest. A distraction. "You must think I'm completely stupid. Now take off your clothes."

"What?"

"You heard me. You wouldn't be the first amateur thief to hide stolen goods in her underwear."

The woman sat bolt upright on the edge of the bed and stared at him open-mouthed for a few seconds. "I'm not taking anything off. Who the hell do you think you are?"

"You don't know? I'm disappointed." Clever, playing the outraged innocent, but he was having none of it. "You can call me *Señor* while we do this. Now take off your clothes, or I'll do it for you."

"If you touch me again, I'll—"

"You'll do what? Scream? Call the police?" Ricardo laughed and took a step closer, bending so that his face was close enough to see flecks of gold in her irises. It wouldn't be the first time a corrupt police officer was in league with a petty criminal either, so he was taking no chances on what she may have already stashed away. "They'll be here soon enough. Once I've finished with you …"

Her eyes were wide and clear. "Just promise me you won't hurt the Condesa if I agree to do what you say."

"The Condesa?" What was the little crook up to now? Not that it mattered, but it would be nicer not to have to wrestle her to the ground before the police arrived. He took a long breath and allowed his gaze to drop to her mouth as she stood up to face him. "Very well, we'll leave the Condesa out of it."

"We can be civilized about this." The blonde licked her lips and her voice dropped an octave, becoming silky as she fingered his collar. "What *is* your name?"

Ricardo suppressed the urge to laugh. The little minx was trying to seduce her way out of trouble! "Take off your clothes," he said firmly and then everything went black with pain.

• • •

"You're an oaf, Ricardo," Condesa Antonella Almanza muttered with an expression as sour as green lemons. "The poor girl thought she was about to be raped and murdered up there. I expect you to apologize when she brings our coffee."

Ricardo rose from a white leather sofa and thrust his hands deep into his trouser pockets. His stepmother never failed to irritate him. "Perhaps, dear *madrastra*, you would care to explain to me what that English woman is doing here in the first place? Apart from making coffee, fetching your jewels, and kicking like a rabid mule, that is."

"And perhaps you would like to explain to me what you were doing sneaking around upstairs without permission?"

"I own the place, remember?"

She frowned and ran a beautifully manicured hand over her shiny black hair.

"Helen Marshall is my Girl Thursday."

"Your what?" Ricardo said with a laugh of disbelief.

"The same as a Girl Friday, only faster." The older woman sniffed disdainfully, unwilling to look him in the eye. "It's all about one's work-life balance."

Ricardo shook his head. "You kill me with your mad ideas, Antonella. You really, really do."

She picked at an invisible speck on her Chanel jacket. "You don't understand my needs, you never have."

"Your needs? I think I've got a pretty good idea by now, judging by the accounts I approve for payment every month."

"I need to relax more, have some 'me time.'"

"Give me strength! What do you do all day? You have a cleaner, a cook, a gardener—"

"How dare you! I gave your father the best years of my life. He and your wretched family ruined me for anyone else. He owed me for that, and as a consequence, the debt is now yours, as eldest son."

"The *only* son," he snapped. "And I have never dishonored that debt. So how much are you paying this little English cuckoo?"

Helen Marshall coughed politely in the doorway, noting the fury on the Condesa's face. She'd understood every word of their blazing row. "Your coffee, madam," Helen murmured as she entered the salon, eyes lowered to the Turkish rug beneath her feet.

"Ah, at last." The Condesa replied and waited as Helen poured the coffee with shaky hands. She took her cup carefully, so as not to tangle her nails in the tiny handle and jerked her chin towards the man Helen now knew was Ricardo Almanza. "Before you go, my appalling stepson has something to say."

Helen took a step back from the coffee tray and slowly raised her face, catching her reflection in an elaborate mirror over the fireplace. She looked pale, her makeup having been partially rubbed off on the Condesa's bedspread. She could no longer avoid acknowledging the tall shadow hovering to the far right of her vision. Ricardo Almanza's aura dragged her eyes to meet his once again. The angry stare she remembered boring into her in the bedroom was the same, just calmer. His eyes were the color of Baltic amber, his hair as black as night and a trace of the mandarin and persimmon in his cologne hung in the still air. Gold cufflinks in the shape of a lion's head glinted on the white shirt cuffs protruding from his black jacket. His fingernails were short and clean and a shiver ripped through her as she remembered the feel of his hard hands gripping her…

"I owe you an apology, Senorita Marshall. My behavior was unfortunate. I felt compelled to protect my stepmother from an intruder. I had not been informed of your employment. I made a mistake."

Tall, dark, and angular, he would tick all the boxes if he wasn't such a misery. "And I'm sorry I kicked you so hard in the—I apologize for being so vicious," she said, recalling the ferocity with which she'd slammed her foot into his groin.

A slow smile changed his countenance entirely and a lump formed in her throat.

"You were frightened, it was understandable."

"Yes. Yes I was," she murmured. No air moved and the atmosphere was heavy as a clock chimed five times. She gritted out a smile. "Will that be all today, madam?"

"Going so soon?" Ricardo interjected before the Condesa could answer. "Please, there's something I'd like to know before you go. What exactly did you do here today?"

"Do?" Helen switched to the Condesa, silently pleading for guidance. She was sure her employer didn't want her stepson to know what happened most afternoons during siesta.

"Yes, fulfilling the terms of your contract, you know, earning your pay." He shot a scornful glance at his stepmother and appeared to ignore the vitriol in her expression.

"Well, um, today we started learning Mandarin," Helen said brightly.

"Mandarin? Is that so?" Ricardo slapped the back of the sofa. "Well, well, well that's going to be so *incredibly* useful when you go handbag shopping in Milan, Antonella. How forward thinking of you. I am so very, very impressed."

"Shut up, Ricardo," the Condesa snapped. "I have every right to expand my mind and improve my education."

"You certainly need to," he muttered.

The Condesa shot him a look of contempt. "And before you complain and penny-pinch for one more second, I absolutely refuse to let her go until I can speak some basic Russian as well. So essential these days."

"What a waste of money."

Helen simmered with indignation. It was bad enough being employed as an overqualified slave to a spoiled and vain old woman, but to be discussed like this was insulting.

They were behaving as if she didn't exist! She straightened her spine and lifted her chin. She'd heard quite enough of their bickering. "If that will be all today, I'd like to catch the next bus home. I'll have to wait another two hours if I miss the five-thirty down to the harbor."

"Harbor? You are not staying in the staff wing?" He turned on his stepmother before Helen could reply. "Please don't tell me you've filled the whole villa with staff dedicated to your 'wellness.' I didn't think it would be possible to pour any more money down the drain."

"I choose to live out," Helen said. "It means I can bring nice fresh things for her from the market each day on my way here. I haven't asked for an increase in salary to reflect this arrangement, so there's a cost saving, a matter close to your heart, it appears."

Ricardo stood silently for a moment, and then raised a sardonic eyebrow. "Why Ibiza town? You don't like luxury villas with spectacular views and oligarchs as neighbors?" He lazily ran a fingertip across his chin. "Or maybe it's because you enjoy being herded like cattle on public transport twice a day?"

"I love this villa," Helen replied sharply. That was twice he'd likened her to an animal, the arrogant sod. "But the current living arrangement suits us both well."

More silence. She may have gone too far.

"Fair enough." He took a set of car keys from his trouser pocket and smiled again. His teeth were as white and perfect as the Condesa's best pearls. "It's probably more fun in town anyway, but I won't hear of you catching the bus tonight. I'll see you safely back."

No!

Helen felt her ankles wobble. "No, really. It's not necessary, the bus stop is at the end of the road and it takes me right past my flat." She could sense her face was growing red and shiny with embarrassment. She had to get out of this.

"I insist," he replied silkily, as if he could read her mind. "Unless your boyfriend would disapprove?"

"No. Of course not," she said crossly. "I don't need a boyfriend to look after me. I'm capable of doing that myself."

"Do you do *everything* yourself, Helen Marshall?" Ricardo asked in a soft voice that made the hairs on the back of her neck stand on end. She knew exactly what he meant by that remark, and a sudden flutter low in her pelvis warned that she was far from being affected by him. Whether she liked it or not, the man oozed sex. He was dangerous and enticing, a brooding presence that put ordinary men in the shade.

"That's quite enough, Ricardo," the Condesa snapped. "Take the poor girl home and behave yourself. We've both had quite enough of you today."

Helen reluctantly followed Ricardo through the salon door. She should have put her foot down about the lift. She was walking into big trouble, but she couldn't stop herself. She was being drawn in his wake, helpless, like a moth to a flame...

It was a peculiar sensation, leaving the villa through an elaborate arch that led to a paved courtyard. Before now Helen had always come in and out through the back entrance by way of the kitchen and utility areas, a situation appropriate to her role in the household and with which she felt quite comfortable. Still more peculiar was the sparkly sensation zinging around the inside of her forehead. Trailing Ricardo Almanza's exquisitely muscled behind was probably shortening her lifespan by a few good weeks. He wore a suit well.

The light was rapidly fading into a slumberous Mediterranean evening, and the white stone walls of the villa glowed in a way that reminded her of the moonstones on her mother's eternity ring. The courtyard lemon trees were now black silhouettes against a violet and pink sky, and she remembered why she loved this part of the world so much. Heat, color, the sizzle of insects.

Ricardo turned into the narrow road outside the villa's walls and Helen stopped dead in her tracks behind him. "Don't tell me that thing is yours."

"*Si*. Of course it is. What did you expect? A cheap Spanish car, like a SEAT?" He glanced at the red Ferrari and shrugged. "It's a cliché, but I like fast cars."

Helen nodded slowly and feigned a sigh. "And there I was expecting a moped ride."

His chin jutted upwards and the movement of an eyebrow muscle was sufficient warning for her to say no more. "I wouldn't expect *any* woman in my company to straddle one of those things." His eyelids lowered. "They have me for that."

Helen blushed and was glad of the fading light. *Talk about shameless ego.* She tossed her hair belligerently and silently slid into the passenger seat.

"You've got to admit this is more fun than the bus," Ricardo said a few minutes into the journey.

"I guess ..." Helen clutched the door trim as he took a sharp bend and sounded his horn at a truck carrying oranges. She swallowed hard and stared pointedly out of the window. He didn't need to see how he was affecting her equilibrium. It wasn't his driving either. Each time he thrust the Ferrari into another gear, his trousers pulled tightly over firm thigh muscles and she could feel the heat of his body in the snug confines of the car. Sharp darts of awareness unexpectedly pulsed between her thighs and she was shocked at how difficult it was proving to suppress them. His scent was good too—the cologne she'd smelled earlier had complex layers and was crammed with pheromones. She squeezed her eyes shut and tried to pretend he wasn't there. What was the matter with her? He had all the hallmarks of a first class jerk.

"Don't worry," Ricardo said as his long fingers tapped impatiently on his knee. "We're just coming onto a straight bit, so I can speed up."

"Oh, good," Helen said looking warily across at his angular profile. "How long until we're back in town?"

"About ten minutes." He flicked through at least three gears before she could even gasp. The bus took about half an hour.

"Don't rush on my account."

He grinned and looked straight ahead before flooring the accelerator.

The sensation was like being struck from behind by a runaway juggernaut. The engine roared, its power prickling the soles of her feet as they shot along the peninsula. She couldn't help admiring how the mechanical beast submitted to its master's touch, fluidly cornering each sharp bend. It was thrilling. It was dangerous.

This was the second time today she had faced the prospect of an untimely death, and on both occasions at the hands of Ricardo Almanza. The sooner she could get out of this car and away from him the better. She didn't have time to die on Ibiza, and more to the point, she couldn't afford to. She didn't like the effect he was having on her. She had much more important things to do than indulge in wild fantasies involving Spanish playboys.

"So, tell me," Ricardo suddenly said, his voice raised above the throaty roar the engine. "What brings you to work in Ibiza?"

"Oh this and that. It's a beautiful part of the world." She felt a surge of relief as she spotted a sign indicating the harbor was just one mile away. The ordeal would soon be over.

"How long are you here for? Six months or so? What's the deal?" After a few seconds of silence, Ricardo gestured with a hand that he was waiting for an answer.

Helen sighed. She had nothing to lose by telling him. "I came over last season with some friends. I needed a break. I liked it and decided to stay for a while. It wasn't planned from the outset. I had a few jobs, office work, bars, and when my last contract was terminated I needed to get a better-paid job quickly. I got lucky, and an agency came up with the position for your stepmother. The money was so good I said yes immediately."

Ricardo nodded thoughtfully. "How long is your contract?"

"We agreed to work on a week to week basis," Helen said cautiously. "I guess she needs to be sure that I'm up to the job. Although I've made it clear I probably won't stay any longer than six months. I should head back to England after that."

"It's all about the money then?" Ricardo said as he carefully inched the Ferrari through the narrowing streets of Ibiza town.

"It's amazing here, and I'd love to stay for lots of reasons, but I have responsibilities back home." Her thoughts jettisoned back to the ungodly mess waiting in England and her resolve stiffened. Her own dreams would have to wait. "So, yes, it's all about the money for now. It has to be."

Ricardo slowed the car to a crawl and looked quickly left and right. "Where to next?"

"You can drop me here and I'll walk the rest of the way. I'm just off Calle Manuel round the corner, it's not far."

"No, I'll take you to your door. It's dark," he said and kept on driving.

Helen smiled and unzipped her handbag. "Ibiza town is never really dark and your car won't fit in the road outside my place, it's too narrow." She found her house keys and rattled them in her fingers. "Don't worry, I'll be fine."

"Humor me. I won't sleep from worry if I don't see you safely home."

"So gallant." She pointed to the left. "Just there, by the postbox. It's as close as you're going to get."

Ricardo pulled up, killed the engine, and took the keys out of the ignition. "I'll walk you to your door."

"No," she said firmly. "I can look after myself and you've done more than enough already. But thanks for the lift."

• • •

Helen leapt out of the car and slammed the door shut before Ricardo could argue with her. He watched her briskly walk up a dusty side alley, her golden ponytail catching a few beams of yellow-gray streetlight as she went. It was a rough area, but to his surprise she still waved him away with an agitated hand as he watched her unlock a green wooden door. He was being dismissed! It had to be the first time a woman hadn't asked him in for coffee as well, which made his ego smart.

He didn't give a damn if she was living in a run-down area full of dealers and pimps, being a wealthy man didn't make him a snob. But she didn't know that. All she knew was that he was a flashy relative of her employer who'd tried to strangle her.

God, she was attractive. In spite of the ferocious kick to the groin she'd dealt him earlier, he stiffened below the belt as images of her flashed through his mind. Her full breasts strapped into the passenger seat of his car, and the sway of her hips in the sensible black trousers she'd been wearing taunted him. He drummed his fingers on the steering wheel as his mind began to race.

He wanted her.

He had six months left to get married or lose a long-standing bet and his honor forever. Time was running out.

She wanted money.

He needed a wife.

A plan was taking shape, and he didn't care if he went straight to hell for even considering the idea.

Chapter Two

Helen quickly locked the battered door to her studio flat behind her and slumped against the cold interior wall. She was breathless after racing up three flights of dark narrow stairs. They were far too dank and sinister to hang around in. Perhaps on reflection she had been stupid to agree to living out. This was a dark and dangerous area at night for a woman by herself. She had to admit to feeling genuinely unsafe, but the Condesa had made it obvious that she didn't want Helen living under the same roof as her. Helen knew why—the entire household did—but she was in no position to judge what her employer got up to with her young, buff protégés.

A loud knock on the door shattered the silence and a surge of adrenaline ripped through her. "Who's that?" Helen said. Her hands were trembling. The rent had been paid up two weeks in advance so she wasn't due for an unpleasant visit from her landlord yet…

"It's me.

Ricardo. Open up before I get mugged out here, will you?"

Helen exhaled a tiny laugh, relieved it wasn't her greasy

landlord, and rattled the heavy key in the door to admit a large angular mass of Spanish male. Ricardo slid lithely in before it was even properly open.

"*Dios*, this place is a dump!" He quickly looked around the tiny living room. "How much are you paying for this?"

"It's the cheapest I could find." The half smile on her face disappeared as she followed his eyes around the shabby interior. "I've been waiting for my day off to have a bit of a tidy up."

"I don't think there's much you can do with it, frankly," he said, flicking the flat of his hand roughly across her back.

"Damn!" she exclaimed when she registered what he was doing. "I must remember not to touch the walls. There's bloody paint peeling off everywhere in here."

"It would appear so," he agreed, allowing his hand to rest a moment longer than necessary on her shoulder.

"So, er, did I leave something in the car?" She picked up a pile of mail and pretended she was sorting through it. "It could have waited until tomorrow, I'm sure."

"No, it couldn't. It's been a long day and I'm starving. I wondered if you'd like to go for something to eat."

"Oh." She hesitated a moment. It was a tempting offer. "That's very kind of you, but no, I really—"

"You really planned a lavish meal at home?" He flung open the battered fridge with one hand and a Formica cupboard door with the other sending her a withering look. "A tin of *sardinas*, some rather dubious looking bread, and I'll bet there's not a drop of wine in the place." He slowly closed each door and turned to face her. "I think you just ran out of excuses, so are you coming or not?"

He had her cornered. And she *was* hungry. "Okay, I'd love to." There was no going back now. "But we split the bill."

"Go halves?" Ricardo sighed and ran a hand through his

dark hair. "Do you think I'm poor? Or mean?"

"Neither," she said flatly with a warning glare of defiance. "I'd prefer it that way, that's all."

"You really are annoyingly independent, aren't you?" He looked around the shambolic kitchen area once again. "As you wish, pay the whole bill if you must, but let's get out of here. I need to eat."

• • •

Helen felt herself being eased through the glazed wooden doors of a small Italian restaurant with Ricardo's large hand at the base of her spine. A thrill ricocheted through her as their bodies came into contact, and she had to sharply remind herself that this was chivalry and good manners. Nothing else.

A jovial man in his seventies noisily embraced Ricardo. "Hey Ricardo! *Il molto tempo nessun vede*! Long time no see!" He reached up and grabbed him by both cheeks and then wobbled his head from side to side between slab-like hands.

"For God's sake, Alfonso, take it easy on the hair, will you? I don't want to end up as bald and ugly as you." Ricardo flinched as the old man cuffed him playfully around the ear.

"No one but an Almanza could speak to me like that and still get a table. You are a very bad boy, Ricardo. You notice I speak the English for you, eh?" He then winked conspiratorially. "Fabiana has been beside herself with excitement since I told her you wanted a table for two. She'd get me with the filleting knife if I sent you away before she got a look at your British girlfriend."

"This is Senorita Helen Marshall. I'm showing her a few of the sights." Ricardo was oblivious to the embarrassment that prickled her face. "And before you and Fabiana get any silly ideas, please be aware that she speaks very good Spanish. You won't get away with anything."

"I also speak Italian," Helen said bluntly.

Ricardo forced a tight smile as they followed their host through the restaurant. "And Mandarin."

Helen was irritated that he hadn't corrected the old man on his "girlfriend" assumption. No doubt Ricardo was so self-absorbed he hadn't even noticed her squirm, but she slipped politely into the chair he held out for her. Their table was in a discreet corner. The place had a homely feel with copper pans on one wall and a hodgepodge of faded prints on the other. Tattered Italian soccer posters mingled with an eclectic mix of ceramics, and the warm air was heavy with garlic and olive oil.

"I assume it *is* Senorita?" Ricardo asked quietly. "It was presumptive of me, but Alfonso can be quite a nuisance when it comes things like that. If he thought for one second I was out with a married woman he'd have slung us into the street."

"Has that happened before?" Helen whispered in alarm.

Ricardo dipped his chin and leveled his sharp eyes with hers. "I don't *do* married women." His expression was serious. "So am I safe?"

"Yes," she said firmly. Ricardo poured her a glass of red wine from a stubby carafe. Finding it impossible to maintain eye contact with him any longer, she took a sip from her glass. "Presumably Alfonso's moral code extends to both parties?"

"If you're asking me if I'm married, then the answer is a definite no." He leaned back into his chair and smiled lazily. "Would you be here if I was?"

"I don't see why not," Helen said brightly. "We're only having dinner. It's not as if anything sordid is going on between us, is it?"

"No, no it isn't."

For the next hour Helen enjoyed a selection of the day's

special dishes, made to order using the freshest seasonal produce from the market each day. Helen nibbled first on *fragaglie*, deep-fried baby fish, and they were so delicious she ate the lot as Italian opera played subtly in the background. Consequently, she struggled to finish her exquisitely charred pizza. Ricardo had no such difficulty and not only demolished his pizza, but managed to finish a steaming bowl of pasta and a whole *mozzarella di bufala* as well.

"Dessert?" he said as Helen dabbed her napkin to her lips.

"You're kidding. I'm fit to burst."

"I can see you need some practice when it comes to eating five course meals. It's no wonder you're so skinny."

"Hardly!" Helen said, but was secretly pleased at the compliment. She'd never been skinny, and never would be. Her genes wouldn't allow it.

"Okay, shall we take our coffee outside? It's quieter and less crowded out there." He stood and gestured for her to follow, but not before she saw Alfonso leaning out of the kitchen door, winking at Ricardo. "Ignore the old fool. He's trying to embarrass me. He's been doing things like that since I was a teenager."

The tiny courtyard was surrounded by high stone walls that looked centuries old. It was illuminated by lanterns and a spot-lit fountain that trickled pleasantly in the darkness. The perfume of jasmine flowers and basil filled the night air as she followed Ricardo to a round table.

"It's lovely." Helen closed her eyes in appreciation. "I can't believe we're the only ones out here."

"And I have seen to it that it stays that way," Ricardo murmured.

The hairs stood up on the back of her neck as his eyes fixed her with a strange intensity. "What do you mean?"

"I have a proposition for you, and I don't want it to be the talk of the Balearics by morning. Not until I choose it to be, anyway."

"Go on," she whispered, trying to hide the excitement in her voice.

"You need money, yes?"

"I've already told you that."

"You didn't tell me how much though, did you?"

Helen began to feel nervous. "It's not any of your business."

"It could be."

"I'm not following you, Mr. Almanza, and I now think it's time I went home."

"You can't possibly call that hovel down the street home. And the other place? The place you call home in England? You can't go back there until you've put your hands on enough money to satisfy whatever squalid needs you have there. I've deduced that much."

"How dare you! You know nothing about me or my circumstances."

"Maybe not, and I'm not the least bit interested in your life in England, but you need money fast and I've got lots of it."

"So? Am I supposed to be impressed?"

"Please be quiet and listen. I *also* need something quickly, and I think you're the perfect person to help me out."

Helen went to get up. She wanted to walk away from the bizarre discussion. She'd heard enough. "This conversation is over."

"I will pay you one million euros if you agree to work with me for three months."

Her hands froze on the tabletop. "As *what*, might I ask?"

"As my wife."

Helen stared at him in horror for a second, and then she began to smile. "Oh, very clever. How long did it take for you to cook that joke up with Alfonso? Was it when you were quietly discussing the house red? Or was it when I went to the loo? Well, I must say I'm relieved, because for one awful moment I thought you'd brought me out here to sell me a dodgy franchise. Or a timeshare."

"I am serious."

"Yeah, sure you are. I might be unsophisticated, but I'm not a complete fool."

"Let's hope not, because I get very tired of the sound of my own voice saying the same thing over and *over* again." He leaned forward across the table, his fingertips pressed together in a tent shape. "My offer is genuine. A marriage in name only for, say, three months and you get one million euros. Go away and think about it for twenty-four hours. Don't say another word now or you may regret it. Believe me, I do deals like this all the time."

"I'll just bet you do," she said, pushing her coffee cup with a scraping noise to the center of the table. "I can only begin to imagine what sort of a woman you think I am, but don't expect things to go your way this time. I'm not one of the local whores you can pay to do your bidding."

"You do me a disservice. I'm only marrying to satisfy an outstanding matter of honor, not to slake some perversion, and you're perfect for the job. Attractive, intelligent, the perfect trophy wife."

"You can't be serious."

"You also want to leave for home within six months, divorced by then obviously, so we both win. This is a once in a lifetime offer. The last thing I want to do is get married, but I need to before I'm thirty or I'll lose a long-standing bet. A very big bet."

"A bet? My God, you really are as shallow as a puddle. I can never see a time where I'd willingly enter a contract of marriage with such an arrogant, spoiled, and insensitive man. The only way I'll ever consider marriage is when I fall in love, so the answer is no. Double plus no. And now," she said with a flourish as the chair tipped over behind her, "I'm leaving."

.

Early morning sunshine cut through the dirty windowpane and seared across Helen's eyelids. She had slept badly, and as she forced herself out of bed, the nausea of extreme fatigue washed over her. She eyed the magnum of champagne Ricardo had quietly left outside her door the previous night. The expensive bottle looked extremely out of place on the aluminum sink, and memories of shouting at him to leave came flooding back. She shook her head and groaned, realizing the events of the night before really hadn't been a dream.

Ricardo Almanza must be out of his arrogant mind thinking he could pay her to marry him! The idea was ridiculous, and he certainly had too much time and money on his hands if he spent his life getting involved in bizarre wagers. He'd even had the nerve to push his flashy business card under the door before he left. She brushed her teeth roughly in the rust-tinged sink, and it wobbled as she turned off the tap. The entire plumbing system was vintage 1960s by the look of it, air bubbles clattering around the building like loose marbles.

While drying her face, her cell phone began to ring and she considered not answering it. "Go away!" she muttered into the towel. It was probably the Condesa wanting her to bring something particular from the market for her breakfast.

It had been goji berries the day before. She'd seen them featured on TV overnight and had become like a woman possessed until she had some.

Helen scooped the cell phone up in one hand and swore as she fumbled and dropped it, buzzing like a hornet, on the floor. "Hello?" She managed to answer calmly and then felt the blood drain from her hands when she heard her mother's strained voice.

"The bank's brought everything forward. If we don't come up with the money in one week, we're out."

Helen's breath caught. "They can't! Not just like that. Can they?"

"Apparently they can." The connection crackled. "We're set to lose everything in five working days time."

"But, Mum, we had six months." Helen squeezed her eyes shut to quell the panic.

"There's nothing to be done now, love," her mother said. "I thought I'd better call you about your things before the bailiffs get hold of them. Your dad and I are running out of places to send everything. Is there a friend who can look after them until you get back?"

There was a moment of silence as Helen sensed her mother was thinking exactly the same she was: *back to what exactly?*

Her head began to pound. "I can't believe they're doing this. Can't we hold them off for another month? Perhaps by then we can find a way to meet the minimum payment—"

"It's too late," her mother blurted. "They won't budge. We have to accept the inevitable. If there was any hope I wouldn't be ringing you like this."

Helen fisted her free hand to stop it shaking. "How's Dad taking it?"

"Not so good. The doctor upped his heart pills yesterday."

Her mother's voice sounded distant. "He blames the whole mess on himself."

"He was only trying to protect us, Mum."

"I know, darling, but if we'd known the legal fees would eventually outstrip the value of our land and property we'd have given in to the Skiptree Estate's demands a lot earlier. At least that way we would have something left, somewhere to live at least. But we don't have enough cash to fight the court case any longer. We have to give up."

"And let that Skiptree woman bully us until she gets what she wants?" A hot tear slid over her bottom lashes, and Helen wiped it angrily away. "We can't let her drive us out of our home!"

"Pride comes at a too high a price, I'm afraid. Not only has Lidia Skiptree exhausted every penny we have by dragging out the litigation, she's also started to get to our customers. Orders have dropped off, and now, well, we simply can't continue. Even if sales bounce back, we can't afford to implement the latest health and safety requirements that were thrown at us last week. The sterilizing equipment's packed up and we have to pour the milk down the drain." Her mother's voice rose a pitch. "She's got us just where she wants us— reduced to selling a few eggs at the gate."

"Damn the woman," Helen snapped. "What idiot said money can't buy you happiness? It's getting her just about everything her dark little heart wants, even down to that ludicrous off-the-shelf title. *Lady.* She's the furthest you could get from one. She's a monster."

"We aren't the only ones." Her mother sniffed. "She's railroaded the sale of at least three other farms since she came back down from London. She's determined to push this development of hers through."

"Oh no …"

"We can't fight her anymore. I'm sorry, my darling, but we have to face facts. It's over."

"No it isn't, Mum." Helen scraped the back of her sleeve over her sore eyes. "I won't let her do this. It's about time someone stood up to her and gave her a taste of her own medicine. There has to a way we can save Primrose Farm, and I'm going to do everything I can to give Lidia Skiptree a bloody nose."

The line fell silent for a few seconds. "Don't come rushing back, Helen. There's nothing that can be done at this late stage, and I've already started packing things up anyway. You're young and free and shouldn't be having to worry about all this. You should be having fun, not looking out for your foolish old parents."

"I think we can still sort this mess out, I really do." Helen looked over to the business card next to the champagne bottle and swallowed hard before squeezing her eyes shut and crossing her fingers. "Look, I know this isn't the best time to mention it, but I've met someone. He's Spanish. His name's Ricardo."

•

"So you've come to your senses." Ricardo lounged in an armchair on his stepmother's terrace, his long legs stretched out in the sun. "I thought you'd put up some resistance for a day or two, but I'm pleasantly surprised that you've come round to my idea so quickly."

Helen calmly picked up the glassware on the table and loaded it onto a tray. She was grateful there was no way he could hear how hard her heart was beating. "You're assuming I came out here specifically to see you and not just to clear away the remains of last night's cocktail party. Some might call that arrogance."

He looked up from his newspaper and smiled coldly. "Do I assume correctly, or is it time to start turning the screw a little? If I was sensible I'd start reducing the fee by a hundred thousand for each day you make me wait."

She put the tray down on the table. "I wouldn't risk it, Ricardo. You might end up looking a bit silly."

"Might I? How so?"

"Because the fee has gone up. I want two million, and I'd like half of it paid up front within five days."

He was silent, and his stern tiger-eye gaze flashed dangerously until she was forced to turn away. Clasping her hands tightly under her armpits, she stared out over the balcony at the panoramic view of Ibiza town below. A blistering heat haze shimmered over the rooftops and the piercing blue sea made her squint. "Cat got your tongue?" She felt like sandpaper was lining her mouth.

"Not only has she got my tongue, she seems to be after all the cream as well. What a greedy girl you're turning out to be."

"Well, I figure that if I have to marry you, I might as well make it worth my while. I doubt if it will be an experience I'll want to repeat. In that way I'm a lot like you, a loveless marriage isn't something that's ever interested me." Helen could hardly believe what she was saying. "So we can be quite business-like about the whole thing. I will marry you, in three months it will be annulled, and I will disappear from your life forever."

"Not quite." His chair scraped back and within seconds she felt his presence close behind her. "You doubled the price. So the small print changes."

She suppressed a shiver. "Meaning?"

"For two million, I want more. A lot more. There will be no

annulment. The only way our marriage will end is in divorce." She felt his large palms close around her shoulders, and a finger began to stroke the soft flesh on the side of her neck. "My inflated ego could never stand the public humiliation of an annulment. Our union will be consummated."

"You've got to be joking."

He turned her to face him, his smile hard and merciless as he began to twirl a lock of her hair around his forefinger. "You walked straight into very deep water trying to out-bargain me, Helen. It's annoyed me. You will walk up the aisle, smiling as if your life depended on it, and then share my bed. For three months you will be my beautiful, obedient, compliant, willing wife in every way imaginable."

"I won't!"

"You will," he murmured, pulling her tightly against his hard body. "Because you won't be able to help yourself."

His mouth easily silenced her protest. She felt the power in his muscles as she grabbed at his biceps to push him away, but her own arms became weak as the kiss intensified. His tongue explored as he held her tight and her struggle grew half-hearted as she found herself responding to him. Warm lips, sharp stubble, her breasts crushed against his broad chest—she shouldn't let him...

His hands skimmed her bottom, and pulled her so close she could feel the hard ridge of his erection. Head spinning, she touched the bare triangle of flesh below his throat and the shock of such intense awareness made her lungs freeze.

Ricardo drew his mouth away. "I knew you'd see sense, but we mustn't spoil our wedding night by getting carried away." He lightly touched her breasts through the thin cotton of her T-shirt, brushing her tight nipples with the pads of his thumbs. "It will be worth the wait, I promise you."

Helen's eyes opened to find him grinning down at her.

He had her exactly where he wanted her now that her body had been so treacherous. She'd gone up in flames the minute he'd touched her, and the ache between her thighs was like nothing she had ever experienced. Desire. Raw animal desire, but he wouldn't get the better of her. She was no whore.

"I won't sleep with you. It's not going to happen."

"This afternoon, my lawyer will come with the paperwork," he whispered throatily, his breath feathering along her jaw. "And I'm considering making you an appointment with my doctor."

"Your doctor?"

"Yes." He eased away and gripped her shoulders firmly. "I need to be sure you are clean before I sign my money away, don't I? There's no way of knowing where you've been before."

"How dare you!" Helen gasped, flicking away his hands with the sides of her wrists. "How bloody dare you speak to me like that. As if I'm dirt."

"You must see it from my point of view—"

"Then get your damn lawyers to write it into a clause!"

He cocked his head to one side, showing no apparent concern for her wounded feelings. "There's also the matter of contraception. I hate to be crude, but we don't want any accidents prolonging this marriage, do we? I don't anyway. We can't afford to take any risks."

"You're not listening to me, I will not sleep with you, so there are no risks and it's my body, not yours, so I'll do what I want with it."

"In that case, I'll have my lawyers draft a clause to cover that too, because I don't think you'll be able to resist temptation and I never leave anything to chance. Three months and we both go our separate ways." He ran his fingertips along the square ridge of his jaw. "We'll be thoroughly sick of each other by then."

"You can't force me to agree to any of this."

"I wouldn't dream of forcing a woman to do anything." His expression was dark, his slow smile lethal. "If you don't like the terms and you don't want the money after all, then… walk away."

"This is monstrous!"

"This is a business deal that's very much skewed in your favor, so you'd be advised to stop complaining and hand in your notice here immediately."

"I can't! I have to give a month's notice. I'll lose my reference—"

"Then I'll sort this little problem out for you too as we have no time to waste. I'm astonishingly kind after all, don't you think?"

"You're mad."

"And once we've dealt with Antonella I need to pay someone a visit, tell him our good news. He'll be so pleased…"

"So you have at least two *friends*?"

"This one's more of an acquaintance. The guy who bet me I'd never settle down and marry before I was thirty." He laughed to himself. "Want to come along for the ride, or wait until the big day before you meet?"

"I'll pass on that."

Ricardo turned his head to look at her and smiled like he'd been injected with Botox—cold and without genuine expression. "Of course…you're still employed to clear up Antonella's mess until I secure your release, aren't you? You'd better be a good girl and get all this stuff to the kitchen then." He flicked a hand towards a congealed-looking Margarita. "It's attracting flies."

•

Helen watched a mosquito hover around the mirror for a few seconds, and as soon as it strayed over the tiled bathroom backsplash she swatted it with the back of her hand. She noticed that cold bathrooms had a certain smell to them, and a silent, still aura. A sanctuary. But only for a few moments. Ricardo was waiting for her to join him and the Condesa by the pool. Bloody Marys at eleven with pimento almonds. The Condesa loved that ritual. Sometimes it was cashews and Fino sherry, but always at eleven once the hairdresser had finished and left.

Helen would have preferred to do the whole resignation thing alone, but her reason for leaving was so preposterous, so bizarre, she didn't think the Condesa would believe her. Ricardo could deal with the utter insanity of their deal. He was presumably unhinged enough to pull it off without a second thought. She glanced at her reflection in the mirror just as she had the day before. She looked the same, yet harder, as if liquid steel had been injected into her veins. A glaze of ice had layered over her eyes. She had sold her soul to the devil with this fake marriage deal, but she had no choice if she was to save everything she had ever loved. There were mirrors all over the villa, like eyes, windows into the soul asking who was the fairest of them all? There was no question—Antonella, the wicked witch. Only sycophants need apply for Helen's job once she'd gone.

"Oh, there you are!" the Condesa said in a sing-songy voice when Helen approached the pool. "But empty handed?"

"Er, yes."

"But it's eleven o'clock, dear."

"Yes, I know but—"

"We have something to tell you, Antonella," Ricardo said with a voice so calm it made her shiver. He did "in control" so well. He'd be a terrifying enemy. Maybe that was why her heart was pounding so hard. She didn't need another enemy. She didn't need a husband, either, except…bizarrely, now she did.

"Something to tell me?" Her tanned crepe chin wobbled as she twisted a string of pearls between her fingers. "Intriguing…"

"Helen and I are to be married, so she will be leaving your employ with immediate effect."

The Condesa rolled her kohl-rimmed eyes to the sky and made an inelegant snorting noise. "How preposterous."

"Make no mistake, *madrastra*," Ricardo replied, his voice diamond hard. "We are engaged. We will be married quickly. There will be minimal fuss."

"Fuss?" The Condesa's black eyebrows arched like a cat stretching. "You're an internationally renowned Lothario, you stupid boy. Of course there will be fuss! And speculation…"

"I can deal with that."

"I would ask whether your new fiancée is with child, but considering you only met yesterday—"

"I'm not pregnant," Helen said. "We've not even—"

"We've not even set a firm date or venue." Ricardo took Helen's hand in his. "And I need to ask her father for her hand, so we'd appreciate your discretion for now."

"My discretion?" The Condesa blinked and took a long breath before fixing Helen with a cold stare. "Naturally, discretion."

"Excellent. So would you like me to replace your Girl Thursday, or is that something you'd like to arrange yourself?"

"I'm not senile if that's what you're inferring. What I need right now is a Bloody Mary."

"Perhaps I can fix it for you one last time?" Helen shot Ricardo a pleading look.

"That would be most welcome." The Condesa sent a

sharp glance in Ricardo's direction. "You've just perfected the mix. I'd appreciate it."

Ricardo paused, took his phone from his pocket and checked it before saying, "Very well. I have an important call to make anyway. Say your farewells. Helen, I'll be in the car when you're finished."

He turned on his heel and the two women watched him disappear through a stone arch in the direction of the courtyard where his car was parked.

The Condesa's voice had an edge to it Helen hadn't heard before. "Do you think you can handle him, Helen?"

"I'm not sure. I guess I'll have to."

"You're smart. I think you probably can if you want to badly enough."

"You must be shocked."

The Condesa shrugged. "For a moment I was, but then I remembered he's just like his father—impetuous, impulsive."

"He is?"

"His father proposed to me within three hours of us meeting for the first time. Said it was love at first sight. Such behavior must be genetic."

"I see."

"No you don't," she said sharply. "But no matter. Can I give you some advice?"

The Condesa's advice was the last thing Helen wanted, but she was determined to part on good terms. "I would welcome it," she said quietly.

"I've no idea what's going on between you two, and I don't want to know either, but I'm not stupid. Protect yourself financially and emotionally. Men bore easily and we women age in the end. He'll drop you like a stone when he's had enough, so make sure he buys you plenty of jewelry to see you through your old age." She lifted her hand and admired the large emerald glinting on her middle finger. "And don't fall in love with him, whatever you do. Almanzas destroy their lovers given half a chance. Believe me, I know."

• • •

Ricardo watched Helen turn the key in the lock of the green door to her flat once more. This would be the last time he'd leave her here to fend for herself. Their impending marriage may be a sham, but he had no intention of allowing her to slip back into the side streets and alleys where feral cats and other unsavory creatures roamed.

He revved the engine as he pulled off. It was immature, but he didn't care. The noise took his mind off the meeting he was about to have. It was going to be an unpleasant experience, and right now he felt like a child who'd been sent to the headmaster to be punished for something he hadn't done. Sent by a teacher who'd taken a dislike to him for no good reason. His "head teacher" was Jerardo Capella: his father's ex business partner and his enemy.

"I have an appointment with your boss." Ricardo tossed his car keys to the uniformed flunky who'd met him on the steps of an imposing glass-fronted building fenced in by parking restrictions. "It won't take long. Shift the car if the police take an interest, will you?"

He didn't wait for an acknowledgment before taking two steps at a time and shoving his way through a rotating glass door. He stalled the open-mouthed receptionist by saying, "I'm seeing Capella. He's expecting me. I know where to find him and I'll take the stairs. I'm faster than the elevator." Ignoring her protests he was on the third floor within a minute and turning the handle of a heavy wooden door.

"So it's true," said a white-haired man sitting behind

an enormous desk opposite a panoramic view of the Ibiza harbor. "I had assumed it was some kind of practical joke when my secretary said you wanted to see me."

"This is no joke." Ricardo crossed his arms and glowered down at the older man.

Jerardo Cappella slowly lifted his head, his face showing no emotion. "Then what is so important that you had to come here in person when we both have lawyers to communicate for us?"

"Your wager. I've come to call time on it. I want my father's property back."

A breath of amusement hissed through his nostrils. "The department store, you mean? And those decaying warehouses? I can't imagine why you're so desperate to win the bet and get it all back. You hardly need the income these days, do you?"

"You know damn well it was my father's dying wish that it was reclaimed for the Almanzas. I told you that the day after his funeral, remember? And it was then you refused an offer of millions to hand it over and turned the whole matter into a childish bet, trivializing his last moments. You were laughing in my face before Antonella's tears were even dry."

The older man nodded and smiled. "But, my dear Ricardo, the bet was that you wouldn't be able to abandon your extravagant ways, settle down and wed before your thirtieth birthday. Nothing's changed. I'll only consider signing that real estate back once you're married."

"You stole it from my father in the first place, you bastard."

"That's slander, be careful." He frowned and passed a pen back and forth between his fingers. "Your dear papa was of sound body and mind when he signed those conveyance papers and they were witnessed by two sets of lawyers."

"He signed under duress, Capella, and you promised

you'd get him out of jail if he did. And then you betrayed him."

Capella's fist came down hard on the desk. "Your father betrayed me first, at the same time he betrayed your mother and everyone else who trusted him. He had to pay."

"So that's why you set him up as well as taking his assets? Why you got your gangland cronies to frame him for theft, murder, and fraud?"

"More slander?" The older man stood up, a foot shorter than Ricardo, and cracked a reptilian smile. "There's no proof, and your father was a thief, murderer and fraudster anyway, wasn't he? He'd just never been caught."

Ricardo gritted his teeth and stared at the wall for a few seconds to compose himself. He wanted to pulp the man he'd once considered an uncle. "I'm not here to rake all over this again, Capella. Just get the paperwork drawn up, because I'm getting married. I win the bet."

"But I actually *win*," Capella said, bad teeth filling the gap between his thin lips. "The Almanza playboy heir forced into the institution he despises. The misogynist son shackled to a brood mare against his will. You're *settling down*… It will make you the most miserable man in Spain."

"And that will bring you joy?" Ricardo shook his head. "What did I ever do to you to deserve such hatred? There was once a time when you treated me like your own son."

"That time ended when your father took everything I loved. The sins of your father are being visited upon you, Ricardo. It's my last act of revenge on him." His dark eyes clouded over and he looked away. "I will attend your wedding and then it's over between us. My honor and dignity will be restored. For what it's worth, your torment will bring me no joy. I did once love you like my own son."

Chapter Three

Helen braced herself as the private jet bounced a couple of times and the wheels hit the rain-lashed landing strip. Her hands gripped the armrests until it came to a halt and she heard the clunk of Ricardo's seatbelt being released. She was furious that they were making this whistle-stop journey to the UK at all, but Ricardo had insisted. She'd hoped to keep her parents in blissful ignorance about what she was about to do, but the only way they were going to get married within days was to do it in Gibraltar. And that meant she had to produce her birth certificate, which inconveniently was in an old shoebox somewhere at Primrose Farm.

"Don't look so worried," Ricardo said cheerfully. "Your parents are going to love me."

Helen stared bleakly out of the window. "I hate to agree with you on anything, but I think in this instance you're right."

The elation in her parents' voices was unmistakable when they had chatted over the phone. The financial crisis that had threatened to consume them had been lifted in a matter of days. Years of struggle and worry had been dispelled, and they sounded like different people. Happy. Free. The advance payment of Ricardo's money had given them their lives back in exchange for three months of sacrifice on her part. But the deception made Helen feel sick to her stomach. She knew the joy she would see on her mother's face would be like stolen goods, not really hers to share or take any pleasure in. But telling them the truth about where the money had come from and why would only make *her* feel better.

The truth wasn't an option, anyway. Ricardo had insisted on this day trip to not only to fetch her birth certificate, but also to give their brief engagement authenticity. It wasn't a coincidence that a mob of paparazzi had been waiting for them at the airport. Ricardo wanted to make the news.

"Oh God," Helen muttered as she saw what was on the tarmac. "Isn't a brand new Aston Martin over the top?"

"Not in the least. You are the fiancée of one of the richest men in Europe now. There are certain standards to be maintained. Enjoy it."

Thirty minutes later the car roared up a steep hill, and the sun burst through a cloud to reveal an astonishing vista. Golden fields of rapeseed, swathes of mauve stone, and green hedgerows formed a patchwork quilt over the rolling landscape. The dark blue sea on the horizon shimmered and glistened, crashing against rugged coves, and a church steeple spiked through a hamlet of thatched cottages clinging to the edge of a silver river.

Helen breathed out slowly. "Home."

Ricardo nodded. "It's beautiful."

Helen smiled and looked out of the window again, avoiding his eyes and the dark contract they were holding her to. If only this engagement was for real… Shocked by her involuntary thought, she immediately locked the notion away in a mental drawer marked "impossible dreams." The very idea was madness, crazy with a side order of delusion. She needed to remember that he was no more than a feckless playboy, a man prepared to marry for the sake of a bet. Determined to win at any cost, he had the morals of an alley cat and would go to any lengths to get his own way. She shouldn't let sexual attraction trick her into thinking there was any depth to the man at all.

It was just before lunchtime when they arrived, which was precisely when Ricardo had insisted they *would* arrive. His network of flunkies had delivered them stylishly and faultlessly to their destination without the slightest hitch or delay, which was a minor miracle at that time of year. Ricardo even seemed to have control over the holiday traffic that usually clogged up the arterial roads to Brackley Bench. He'd dressed for the occasion too. Gone was the sharp suit, and he was now dressed in head to toe designer country casual. Even in stonewash jeans, a grey roll neck sweater and Ugg Rockvilles he was stunning to look at.

The car clattered over a cattle grid at the entrance to Primrose Farm, and a large bird left a calling card on the Aston's immaculate windscreen.

"Welcome to the New Forest." Helen suppressed a giggle as the car came to a stop in the yard. "The wildlife must have seen you coming."

"This place. It smells like…blue cheese," Ricardo said, his brow furrowing with distaste.

"Doesn't it though?" Helen said as she scrambled out of the car. "We call it silage here. But only the cows eat it."

Helen's parents were waiting as they arrived. Broad smiles greeted them on the red brick porch full of old rain boots and kittens. In the herb garden outside, a cockerel puffed out his chest as his hens pecked and fussed around him. Being hugged warmly by both excited parents made her forget her deception for a while, their chatter and animation warmed her inside, but she still avoided eye contact with Ricardo when she introduced him.

"What's for lunch, Mum?" Helen breezed into the kitchen. She had a pretty good idea from the smell that was coming from the old, blackened range. It had been the heart of the home for generations, providing heat, food, and a gathering place away from the hardships of outdoor life. She recognized the smell of homemade steak pie, and judging by the steamed-up windows they'd be having black cabbage and boiled potatoes too. She couldn't wait to see how Ricardo would react to his future mother-in-law's rustic cuisine.

To Helen's surprise and intense annoyance, Ricardo ingratiated himself with her parents effortlessly. He was a master of seduction on all fronts, smooth, entertaining and completely disarming. She had hoped to glean some satisfaction from his being completely out of place. In fact, she'd been particularly looking forward to watching him swallow every mouthful of her mum's "signature" pastry. Cooking was not one of Mrs. Marshall's strengths—unusual for a farmer's wife, but she'd not killed anyone yet.

"Just like the finest *cavolo nero*," Ricardo enthused, piling dark, bitter kale onto his plate. "And organic, even better!"

Her mother glowed. Her father nodded approvingly and opened a big bottle of cider, which was an honor, indeed. Ricardo looked as if butter wouldn't melt in his mouth as he munched his way into her parents' affections. He was infuriating. And he had the most tempting mouth.

Helen was close to throwing up when her mother declined Ricardo's second offer to wash up. "No, no!" she trilled. "Why don't you show Ricardo around, Helen? I hear there's an egret nesting down on the marsh somewhere. You don't see many of those."

"Okay, that sounds like a very good idea." She'd had quite

enough of the happy extended family scenario. It was time to play dirty. She didn't much care if Ricardo noticed the glint in her eye as she picked up a big smelly pair of muddy boots. He'd bloody asked for it, being so disgustingly well mannered and charming around her mum. She wanted to see him squirm. "These are for you. *Darling*."

"That went well," Ricardo said as they trudged uphill towards a wooden stile on the edge of a meadow. "Your parents seem to like me. We make a convincing pair."

Helen shot him a cold look. She'd felt like a fight since dessert and was delighted that he hadn't noticed her kick a streak of wet manure up his back when he wasn't looking. "We're alone now, so you can stop acting as if you're actually a nice person. Having said that, you're really very good at it. Acting that is. It comes with practice, I suppose."

Ricardo stopped walking and let out a hollow laugh. "It baffles me how people as nice as your parents managed to produce such a misery for a daughter. It doesn't seem biologically possible somehow. What made you so sour?"

"You."

"What?" He started walking again. "You entered into this agreement willingly. No one held a gun to your head. You appear to need my money more than I need a difficult new bride, however much you turn me on."

Helen felt her cheeks burn as a sharp arrow of sexual awareness found its target. She felt like such a hypocrite. Their rapidly approaching wedding night was never far from her mind. If he could inflame her senses with one brooding flick of an eye, heaven only knew what would happen if she ever let him touch her naked flesh.

"Anyway," Ricardo said swinging his athletic frame over the stile, faded denim stretching tight for a moment over his thighs and backside, "what's the money for?"

Helen hadn't been expecting that question. Ricardo had advanced her half the money, and she'd cleared her parents' debts the same day. She hated lying to them, but had convinced them she'd arranged a new financing package while she was in Ibiza. A long-term deal with a Spanish financial institution, secured on her future earnings.

The deception was horrible, but she could never tell them what she'd really done to get the money. They'd be appalled. Added to that, her father was a proud and independent man. He'd allow his family to pitch in. After all, Helen was an only child and would ultimately inherit, but he'd hate for any one else to know the mess they were in. Rightly or wrongly he would feel ashamed of what he viewed as his failure to protect his assets and family's future. And to be bailed out by his future son-in law? That would be unthinkable.

Helen was clear in her own mind that her parents didn't need to know the truth, and neither did Ricardo. "I don't think that's any of your business," Helen said. "It's not going to fund anything illegal if that's what you're worried about."

"That hadn't crossed my mind at all until you mentioned it. Spiraling debts, was it?"

"Something like that," Helen conceded, in an attempt to satisfy his curiosity.

"Too many designer handbags, eh?" he said mockingly, and cast a glance over the small leather backpack she was carrying. "You women are such suckers."

Helen simmered with fury. She'd never bought a designer item in her life, not even from a charity shop! But she couldn't let him know that. "We all make mistakes," she said in a flustered tone. "Don't try and tell me you haven't, Ricardo. This stupid bet of yours must count as one."

"That's an entirely different situation." His expression was as hard as stone. "A matter of honor, as I told you before."

"Yeah, right." Helen didn't even try to hide the scorn in her voice. "Not some playboy antics that got out of hand after too much beer, then?"

The muscles in his jaw twitched with annoyance as he stared angrily out over the teal and grey estuary marshland. "It's very refreshing here." He poked at a plant with his foot. "What's that stuff down there? I'm sure I've eaten it at The Savoy before, is that possible?"

"Every possibility," Helen said as she picked a little of the fleshy plant for him to try. She studied the sweep of his nose and the way his nostrils flared slightly as he stared at the ground. She'd noticed his sudden change of subject—she'd touched a raw nerve. "It's samphire. Some people call it sea asparagus. It does set off a plate of seafood quite prettily."

"It tastes like the air smells," he said thoughtfully as he studied the slender green plant between his fingertips. "Salt and ozone. Nice. It's a good place here, you know. I could picture a really nice marina development. The views are fantastic and the access to the shipping channels would be a real selling point—"

"You wouldn't be the first to have the idea, believe me."

"Really? Anyone I've have heard of? I do a lot of business over here, mainly in London, but it's a small world."

"*Lady* Lidia Skiptree. She owns a lot of land around here. She also spends most of her time in London from what I can gather. Buying stuff. You may well have bumped into each other in The Savoy," she added with a dry look. "I imagine she'd take quite a shine to you, Ricardo. She has appalling taste."

"You don't get on then?" He rocked back on his heels, the wind whipping his hair into black spikes. "The name isn't familiar, so I don't think we've met. Which is a pity because she sounds fun."

Helen scowled, acutely aware of the flare of indignation she felt at his apparent interest in her. Skiptree, her nemesis. "She'd eat you alive."

"There's no way she could be as bad as one particular Brit that took a shine to me a few years back." He let out a low whistle as he stared into the middle distance. "She'd make your average bunny boiler look like Tinker Bell."

"I rather like the sound of her, in that case. Pity she didn't finish the job."

"Charming." He glanced up at the darkening clouds. "We'd better be heading back. Our flight is scheduled to leave in three hours, and I still have to ask your father for your hand. Do you think they will be happy with their new son-in-law to be?"

"I'm sure they will be delighted."

Helen turned away and sharply marched back down to the farmhouse. She could hear his breath as he followed close behind. It was like being chased to the ground by the hounds of hell. There was no going back on her immoral deal now. Everything in her life was about to change, and the dull ache in her belly grew stronger with every step.

Chapter Four

"Welcome to Casa Colina, one of my Spanish mainland bases." Ricardo gestured towards the enormous building. "Much more private and luxurious than the best hotel in Marbella. And I should know because I own that one too."

He dismissed the white chauffeured Mercedes, and took Helen's arm with the confident touch of a man comfortable in his own skin, master of all he surveyed. There was no denying it was a view to die for. Perched high up over Puerto Banus, the Mediterranean sparkled, and the panorama stretched all the way along the golden coast against a backdrop of dramatic mountains. The house was a slab of blinding white against the deep blues and greens that surrounded it, like a star between sea and sky. It was worth millions. Stepping onto a marble terrace, Helen let the warm breeze fill her lungs, while the Andalucian sun dazzled her eyes and the pungency of Mediterranean herbs tingled her palate.

"Everything has been made ready for our arrival. Will it do for a few days?" Ricardo asked.

"It's amazing, I've never seen anything like it."

Ricardo chuckled. "You have no idea who you're

marrying, do you? There are more houses like this. It's one of the ways I make my money."

"Oh." She touched the waxy petals of a pink hibiscus flower. "So you don't just have a woman in every port. You have a mansion to stick her in as well."

He shrugged. "Enjoy it while you can. Carlos Andretti, the designer, and his people are descending in thirty minutes to start on your dress. Then there's the wedding organizer, so decide what sort of civil ceremony you want. Not to mention the beautician, hairdresser, and holistic therapist my team has organized. You're going to be a very busy woman in the coming days arranging the wedding of your dreams."

"The wedding of my dreams?" Helen laughed bitterly. "Do you want any say? Or is it all up to me?"

"Do what you like." He sighed, which she took as a sign he was becoming bored. "If you can't be bothered or can't cope, I will deal with the arrangements. But going by my experience of women, you'll do a very good job of it with unlimited resources at your disposal."

Helen suddenly felt deflated. Women really didn't feature highly on his list of favorite things, sex aside. "What about your parents? Will they want to vet me? Or am I to be an irrelevance to the entire Almanza family?"

Ricardo ignored her question and strolled towards a wine cooler positioned in the shade of a vine-covered alcove. He grabbed a chilled bottle of Cava and ripped off the gold foil covering the cork, before filling two crystal flutes. Helen watched the froth rise with a frenzy and then subside.

"My mother is dead."

She opened her mouth to speak, but was interrupted before she could offer a condolence.

"And my father is dead." He handed her a glass and took a sip from his own. "I had a brother, who is also dead." His expression was as hard as granite. "That is all there is to say about my family. Your family, your parents, are good people. I like them a lot. Let's make it an occasion for them, yes? You never know, we might get to enjoy it too."

Helen felt her hands, head, and sternum prickle. She suddenly felt cold and nauseous. She managed to put her glass on a side table with a clatter and then swayed towards the balcony.

"Hey!" Ricardo swiftly grabbed her elbow to support her. "I think you need to get some rest."

"No, it's okay, I'll be fine," she replied weakly, annoyed with herself for behaving like a swooning wimp, but also disturbed by her loss of physical control.

Ricardo lifted her effortlessly into his arms and began to head for the inner cool of the house. "I disagree."

. . .

Half an hour later Ricardo stroked a lock of hair from Helen's forehead as she slept. She was very endearing for such a blatant money grabber. "You don't fool me," he whispered. "You're just like all the others." She was after all she could get, but as he watched her eyelids flicker, he suddenly felt bizarrely protective. He wondered what she was dreaming about…

Guilt began to nibble at him. Was he having second thoughts because her parents were being duped? Or was it because she had been maneuvered into a marriage she didn't want?

No. He needed to get a grip. She knew what she was doing, and it was all down to hard, cold cash. She might look above suspicion sleeping like an angel on his bed, but there was no mistaking the black diamond that masqueraded for a heart inside her.

There were distinct advantages in controlling a bank. Conveniently, the parent company of where Helen had her current account was under his majority ownership. He'd been keeping a close eye on it, and noted with interest that the million she'd asked for up front had already been transferred to another high street lender. She must certainly have debts. That wasn't his problem, however, and her financial woes were proving to be advantageous to him. If she needed amounts of such a size and with such urgency, she wouldn't walk out on him before the wedding ceremony. He was also looking forward to three months of pleasuring her luscious body in his bed. The prospect was more exciting than anything he could remember in a long time.

• • •

The doorbell rang insistently causing Helen to awake with a start. Coming slowly to her senses, she registered where she was, and then, to her horror, realized that Ricardo was smiling down on her from the other side of the bed.

"How long have you been here?" she asked sharply.

"About half an hour," he said with a lazy smile. "You were yelling about something. Must have been some nightmare."

"This whole situation is a nightmare," she grumbled and pushed herself into an upright position. She had no recollection of having a bad dream. "So don't be too upset if I snore as well. You might want to rethink the honeymoon arrangements, like separate rooms."

"No way." His reply was slow and deliberate. "You don't get off the hook that easily." The doorbell rang again. "You have to earn the balance of the two million, and you still owe me on the down payment, remember?"

Helen focused on the hollow at the base of his throat, visible above the white collar of his shirt. With the top two buttons left open, his smooth, tanned skin would tempt a saint. She quickly swallowed down a spike of desire. He would be incredible to go to bed with. How could he not to be with a body like that?

"How could I forget?" she said with a croaky voice. "But I hope you won't be disappointed when I remind you that the answer is still no. I will not willingly sleep with you. It could be a pretty dull three months, unless you've planned out the divorce too? Will it be adultery? Yours?"

"Am I really that awful? You never know, being my wife might not be that bad. There are plenty of others out there who would leap at the chance. For free."

She stared belligerently out of the tall window opposite the bed, biting down on her bottom lip. He was right and they both knew it. "You don't need my approval. Your ego's big enough to cope on its own."

Ricardo let out an irritated sigh. "Have it your way. I don't want to make your life any more unpleasant than it has to be, or mine for that matter. And by the way, are you sure you wouldn't like to consult my doctor? I had a chat with him yesterday, on behalf of a 'friend,' and he said an implant's a safe method—"

"You don't *own* me! How about you take some responsibility? I've complied with the terms of your contract and it's dealt with. *My* choice. A method I can stop using the minute our 'arrangement' ends, or even sooner with any luck. I even made sure your lawyers got a certificate proving I've done as you asked. God, you must have a low opinion of me, trapping a man with an unplanned baby is something I would never do under any circumstances."

He was silent, but raised a sardonic eyebrow.

"What would I gain anyway? Your lawyer's got every possible event covered in the pre-nuptial agreement." She shot him a look of venom. "Or do you think I might want a permanent reminder of my lovely time as your wife? An image of the great and gorgeous Ricardo Almanza. I don't want anything from you."

"You want my money."

Helen dared not look him in the eye. She could already picture the dark scowl that her last outburst would have caused, and she had no defense. She did want his money. She needed it.

"So about this wedding," Ricardo said. "I assume you want the works? Tons of white silk, champagne, flowers, confetti. Am I right?"

Helen studied her nails and assumed the most superior tone she could manage. "Who's coming from your side?"

"Is it important?"

"I am vaguely interested, as it happens, yes."

"That's entirely up to you, *querida*. I'm not bothered."

Helen turned her head to meet his amber gaze. "What I'd really like is a quiet, quick affair with the least fuss possible."

Ricardo looked at her as if she was mad. "Seriously?"

"Completely." She looked him coldly in the eye. "It's not as if any of this is real, is it?"

"No. I suppose not." Ricardo shrugged. "Obviously, I have to invite the guy who I have the bet with, Jerardo Capella, and then there has to be at least one more witness."

"The Condesa?"

Ricardo snorted. "Maybe not. She still isn't speaking to me after I stole her best girl. And, anyway, I hate her almost as much as Capella."

"You said it has to be *authentic,* though . It seems a shame that you had to meet my parents and go through that charade to risk having your secret uncovered at the last minute."

"No risk. Quick private ceremonies are becoming increasingly popular with those who value their privacy and don't need the cash from glossy gossip magazines to pay for it all. Especially when the bride is already pregnant."

Helen gasped with horror. "You wouldn't…"

"No need to, darling. We just decline to comment, smile sweetly, and let the gossip mongers make up their own minds. They will come up with outrageous conclusions, don't you worry." He then looked at her thoughtfully. "Are you sure a quiet wedding is what you want?"

"This is just a big game, remember? I'd feel a lot happier if I didn't have to witness my mother's tears of joy."

"So you *do* have a conscience? But what will you tell her?"

"I'll think of something." Helen winced as the doorbell and the telephone started to ring simultaneously. "But please tell all these people to go away, will you? I can't stand it!"

Ricardo leapt to his feet with a large grin. "You have no idea how happy that would make me."

"It'll save you a few quid as well."

"This is for you," he said, tossing a blue velvet box onto the bed before strolling towards the door. He turned to see Helen's nimble fingers flip it open, revealing an enormous diamond and platinum engagement ring inside.

He couldn't decide if her shocked gasp was joy or dismay, and as the doorbell rang again, he didn't really care. It was only money.

• • •

Helen padded barefoot into a blaze of early morning sunshine. On the villa's terrace, Ricardo's broad shoulders dominated the back of a cane chair and the white cotton robe he wore did nothing to soften his masculine angles. His jet-black hair was still wet from showering, and trembled like short reeds in the light morning breeze. Helen was rooted to the spot for a moment as the cool marble floor seeped into the warmth of her soles and she took in the sight of him. She watched as he reached for a coffee cup, long dexterous fingers wrapping themselves around the curve of the porcelain, threading themselves sinuously through the handle. She remembered how he'd done the same with her hair on the Condesa's terrace when she'd sold her soul to him. The memory was still fresh. The way he had kissed her. She shivered in spite of the heat.

"I missed you last night, Helen." His dark head turned slowly as she approached. "I had hoped you'd visit me under cover of darkness, put me out of my misery."

"You did? Sorry to disappoint."

"I took a cold shower." Ricardo pulled out a chair and gestured for her to sit down. "Did you sleep well?"

"Very well, thank you," she lied, and poured herself a glass of orange juice. She shot him a tight smile. "But poor you, obviously." She held his gaze for a second or two as he considered her over the rim of his coffee cup, and then lowered her eyes. His sexual pull was so powerful. The fire in his eyes would make the coldest ice maiden sizzle. She wondered if he suspected that she'd been thinking about him all night too, wondering how she would be strong enough to send him packing if he came to her room. In spite of everything she'd said to him, she knew in her heart that she'd have given herself to him without much persuasion. Her treacherous body burned from wanting him and it was becoming difficult for her to ignore.

"I've been thinking," Ricardo said as he tore a fresh

bread roll between his fingers. "As it's our last day of freedom, I'd like to take you out for the day. Or do you need more time to prepare for the wedding?"

Her wedding day. Helen swallowed her rising anxiety about the coming event. She had chosen a dress and accessories from the selection the designer had offered, and the wedding planner had taken care of all the practicalities. The legal paperwork was in order, and her parents had been very understanding about their wish for a quick, quiet wedding. The Marshalls had no desire to be spread all over the European gossip magazines. All Helen needed to do was ensure she arrived at the town hall by eleven on the day. So what more was there to do?

"I don't see why not," she said with a shrug. "Is it going to turn into some hack photo opportunity?"

"Not until dinner time. Until then we'll take a car with blacked out windows, so you don't even need to put any make up on if you can't be bothered."

She pursed her lips and tried not to feel self-conscious about her bare skin and distinctly mascara free eyes. "I'll do my face in a minute, don't worry. My bag's inside."

"We're only going for a drive up into the mountains to have a quiet lunch and some good air. To settle your nerves, hopefully. I want you to see the view, all the way to Gibraltar and the coast of Morocco if we're lucky." He took another sip of coffee and stared hard at her. "Believe me when I say you're beautiful as you are. Leave the make up off if you want to. You don't need it."

Helen felt peculiar all over again at his silky words, and her skin tingled under the fine silk of her bathrobe. She followed the direction of his eyes as her nipples grew hard and formed sharp peaks through the delicate fabric. Her voice was husky as she sensed he knew exactly what she was feeling. "Yes, good idea. I think we really should get out of the house for the day."

•

The centre of Marbella was a bustling frenzy that evening. As Helen watched the spectacle, a flutter of red silk and a smooth, tanned female thigh on the back of a moped caught her attention. She wondered if the man the young Spanish woman was clinging to was her fiancé. Her eyes were closed and she was smiling as her face pressed in against his shoulder blades. They weren't well off. His faded polo top and battered trainers bore testimony to that, but they still looked happy and carefree. Were they in love? How would the *senorita* in the red dress have reacted if *she*'d been presented with a huge, ostentatious diamond in the last twenty-four hours? Most likely she would be on Planet Delirium, showing it off to anyone who would look, kissing, hugging, and ruffling her coltish lover's dark hair.

So why did she, Helen Marshall, Ricardo Almanza's new fiancée, feel so flat? She knew why, it was obvious, and a small part of her was disgusted that she should have any feelings about the situation at all. She felt horrible because none of this was real. She was no more than a business arrangement to Ricardo—a chattel—a playing card. She twirled the heavy band on her ring finger as she watched the battered moped weave through the orange trees and disappear in the crowds. The metal was smooth and cold, the stone as hard as Ricardo's heart.

"Not hungry?" Ricardo said pushing the remains of his *fritura Malaguena* aside.

The air between them hung as thick and heavy as cold honey. Helen shook her head. "I'm still full after that huge lunch you made me eat."

"You only had a lobster salad. You should eat more."

"I'm fine. Really."

Ricardo shrugged and took a sip of wine. "Anyway, I've seen at least two photographers catch us out in the last ten minutes, so our mission is accomplished. We can head back."

"Mission?"

"The whole object of sitting in La Plaza de los Naranjos in the middle of Marbella, in front of one of the world's best restaurants was to get us *seen*." Ricardo rose from his chair and proffered his arm. "Why do you think that hulking great rock on your finger is so enormous? It can be seen from fifty meters and is unmistakably an engagement ring. That's why I didn't let you choose one. I'd bet my life you'd never agree to something quite so vulgar."

"It sums our whole arrangement up quite well," she said with a glance at her left hand. "Vulgar. I'm surprised you haven't forced me into some inappropriately tight dresses as well."

"Soccer player's wives are not my style, Miss Marshall," he said abruptly, and pulled her by the hand into the crowd outside the restaurant.

"We haven't paid the bill!" Helen shouted over the noise of the street as Ricardo dragged her reluctantly along behind him.

He stopped walking and looked at her in surprise. "You don't need to worry about things like that now." He suddenly pulled her tightly into his chest, his arms trapping her by the waist and he lowered his mouth to her ear. "Judging by how much money you had to ask for when all this began, paying your bills is something you're not that accustomed to anyway."

"That's none of your business."

"As my future wife, it is my business, but just to reassure

you, I never pay in Juanito's. We go back a long way and we have…an understanding. Besides, money is a man's responsibility. A woman's role is to seduce it out of him." He brushed a lock of golden hair from her shoulder and lowered his mouth softly to brush her lips with his own. "And right now, Helen Marshall, you're doing a very, *very* thorough job."

"You're an abysmal chauvinist," Helen whispered crossly, as he pulled her even more tightly into him, crushing her breasts against his chest.

"And if I wasn't so rich, you'd absolutely hate me?"

"I do hate you."

"I can tell." He slid the tip of his tongue under her receptive top lip. "You're making it so obvious."

Helen felt dangerous heat pooling between her thighs. "I should slap you for this."

His voice was a husky whisper. "Then slap me hard, because right now I don't think I can wait until our wedding night."

"You must. Otherwise, it's a breach of contract." Helen shivered as his hand slid beneath her top. "If you don't I'll have to put the price up again."

Her knees were like jelly and the breathlessness of her voice did little to hide the effect he was having upon her. His lightest touch sent her up in flames. "It's just as well the wedding will be sooner than later, then," he whispered against her trembling lips.

"What do you mean sooner?" She wasn't sure if she wanted to hear the answer or not.

A smile creased Ricardo's face as he stroked the bare skin of her back, feathering light strokes around the clasp of her bra. "I've pulled out all the stops on this one. The civil ceremony in Gibraltar is booked and paid for. We will be husband and wife the day after tomorrow."

Chapter Five

"*Prisa*! Hurry up! Senorita Marshall!" Luisa, the wedding planner, panted anxiously. "Senor Almanza does not like to be kept waiting. Not even on his wedding day!"

"Now why doesn't *that* surprise me?" Helen said as the middle-aged woman fiddled with the exotic flower she was fixing onto her hair. She'd felt quite numb all morning, oblivious to the luxurious surroundings of the five star Gibraltar hotel she had been booked into the previous night. She hadn't realized how much she would want her mother there to help her get ready. Since waking early, her feelings of isolation had been acute. Even though she'd been fussed over, fed and preened by the ecstatically excited Luisa for three hours now, it wasn't the same.

Luisa left her to check on the cars. Helen stared at her reflection in a full-length mirror and she thought back to the evening she'd spent with Ricardo in Marbella. The memory of him stroking the palm of her hand in the warmth of the night made her shiver. She was as scared, yet excited, about her wedding night as a real bride would be, which was beginning to worry her. Did Ricardo feel the same way? It was unlikely.

This wasn't a real marriage. It was a cold, hard business deal. Helen crushed her teeth together until her jaw hurt.

She needed to get a grip. Part of her was already out of control, skipping towards her marriage vows. Her subconscious was drifting into a theoretical fantasy of what their children would look like—his dark hair and skin, her blond hair and pale skin, so different from each other. She had to stop it, snap out of this ridiculous behavior. It was an impossible situation, and it was hopeless to imagine any good feelings would come out of their corrupt union. She sank her hands into her hair and gripped hard until the pain seared through her head. The whole situation was turning out to be a mega disaster. It was her wedding day to a gorgeous billionaire. She had no right to be thinking about what it would be like to be his wife for real. She had no right to yearn for anything beyond the financial security she'd extracted from Ricardo. She shouldn't be secretly looking forward to their wedding night.

The sound of a telephone ringing made her come back to reality with a thump, and she suddenly felt cold with apprehension. Thank goodness it was a tiny wedding, but it would still be impossible to avoid this Capella person. She and Ricardo hadn't agreed on a cover story, like how they'd met, how long they'd known each other, the sort of questions you would naturally ask a bride and groom. Where would she stand if he realized that Ricardo had faked the whole thing? She wished now that she had read the small print on the documents she'd signed.

"Senorita! Your mamma is on the phone! Quick!" Luisa rustled through the dressing room door, her thin cheeks bearing a little more color than her usual smudge of rouge.

Helen took the wireless receiver and closed her eyes against the high-pitched, chirping that was audible from at least a couple of feet. "Yes, Mum, I miss you both too. Yes

I'll do my best. Thank you, yes the flowers are perfect. I'm wearing the orchid in my hair." She pressed two fingers against the bridge of her nose as her head slumped gradually forward under the barrage of questions being fired at her. "Photos, yes, I'll get some sent to you as quickly as I can."

Photos!

You couldn't have a wedding without photographs! The sham would be obvious. Had Ricardo thought all this through properly? This had disaster written all over it.

As Helen finally cut the call, Luisa pushed her face around the door. "We go now?" she nodded urgently as encouragement. "You get dressed and come and get in the car? No more lateness?"

"Of course," Helen said softly. "Um, do you have a camera?"

•

Emptiness gnawed at Helen's stomach as the black Mercedes sent for her pulled up outside the Registry Office. Baskets of flowers and freshly scrubbed stonework did nothing to lift her spirits, and Luisa's agitation was beginning to rub off on her. "We're here now, Luisa, and we're only a little bit late."

Helen forced a reassuring smile. The wedding planner visibly relaxed a little. She could guess what was going on in the older woman's head. Even though her charge had been safely delivered to the wedding, she would be fretting until the deed was done.

A bitter twist under her diaphragm reminded her that what she was about to do was madness. As a parade of camera flashes heralded her arrival she wished that her dress was long and white and that she had a trio of giggling bridesmaids. Each click of a shutter and shout from a reporter made her wish that her mum was there to hold her hand, and that her dad was here to give her away. Climbing gingerly out of the car she wished that Ricardo loved her and was feeling anxious that his bride was ten minutes late. Her bodyguard's thick suited arm shielded her from the physical crush of the press pack and she wished she didn't have to go through with this terrible deception. She might as well wish for the moon.

• • •

Ricardo clenched his jaw muscles and checked his watch again.

"Not to worry, Almanza," a snide male voice rang out into the silence. "If she's jilted you, you've still got six months to get hitched, and I get to see you humiliated like this all over again. It seems money and good looks can't guarantee even *you* a loving, faithful bride."

Ricardo felt revulsion roll over him as he turned to stare into the coldness of Jerardo Capella's eyes. "I don't remember either of those words being used in your repugnant deal," he whispered harshly.

"Loving? Faithful? All superfluous, surely?" The man standing next to him sneered and lowered his sunglasses down over his eyes. "Marry before thirty was all I stipulated, and I must say, even thus far, it's been well worth it. Get the vows over and I'll sign. Immediately. It would be cruel to gloat over your discomfort any longer than that. I'm not a monster."

"You are scum of the earth," Ricardo said. "And keep your voice down."

"Almanza blood still owes me for my humiliation," Jerardo hissed. "Your name should be dragged through the streets like stinking rubbish for what happened to me. I curse your family birthright and your heirs. If you're man enough to produce any."

Ricardo swore violently under his breath as Jerardo's high-pitched snigger bounced off the walls. Any gentler feeling the older man may have felt towards him had clearly been suppressed or brushed aside. He squeezed his eyes shut. Helen was now fifteen minutes late, and the official was beginning to fiddle awkwardly with the ledgers and paperwork in front of him. The clerk took off his wire spectacles and rubbed his eyes anxiously and then stared at his polished shoes with embarrassment.

The thud of wood impacting on plaster made all four heads snap around to see Luisa rushing through the doorway. Ricardo felt adrenaline flood his body as she froze like a rabbit in the headlights. The breath held in his chest was beginning to hurt. The whispering, the footfalls, the soft movements, all seemed to be reaching an infinity pitch as Ricardo's hands gripped the back of the administrator's chair. He stared blindly down at the cream and green upholstery, and sent up a prayer to God. Not his god. Any god who would listen would do. He needed his bride here *now*.

Kitten heels clicked on the tiled floor, and when he looked up he saw her staring at him, framed in the doorway. Her eau de nil silk shift dress shimmered across her curves as she began to walk towards him, setting off the rich golden glow of her hair and complimenting the sparkling chartreuse of her eyes.

He'd been furious that she was so late, but the light violet scent she always wore dazzled his senses even at a distance. There had been a real possibility that she wouldn't turn up, or even worse that she'd taken the opportunity to flee overnight. The worry that had left his throat feeling sandpapered wasn't just down to the situation with Jerardo Capella, either. There was now more at stake than their ancient wager.

Ricardo didn't want to spend another night away from Helen. It was crazy of him to feel like that about her so suddenly, but he couldn't help himself. Thoughts of her had invaded his mind the previous night. He hadn't slept a wink, and that had given him far too much time to think. He wanted her, there was no denying it, but shame had finally consumed him at the thought of forcing her to sleep with him. What had he been thinking when he bullied her into that deal? It wasn't about the money—two million meant as little to him as one, but she had *challenged* him in upping the stakes and he just couldn't help himself. His cutthroat business instincts had kicked in and he had as good as demanded that she prostitute herself. He'd made a mistake there, shot himself in the foot, because he wanted her to come to him willingly.

She must think he was a monster—she had good reason. He could fix that, but *later*. For the next ten minutes he needed Helen's full cooperation and he couldn't afford to make any mistakes. His stomach muscles clenched at the thought of the solemn legal commitment he was about to make. A commitment he had made clear to her he wouldn't stand by in three months time. He had never broken a promise in his life, but then that was part of the reason why he was stood there now.

• • •

Helen hesitated when she saw Ricardo in the tiny square salmon-colored room. He was clutching a chair back with knuckles as white as bared bone. There were dark hollows under his eyes and his mouth was set in a hard thin line. His ink-black hair shone from being freshly washed, but was tousled, a sure sign that he had been raking his hands through it, with frustration, probably. And anger. She'd kept him, and the other man, waiting. She held her breath, waiting for him to erupt.

"Let's get this over with," Ricardo muttered as he strode towards her and took her by the hand adding, "And you look beautiful, by the way."

It was nice of him to say so, even if it was an afterthought and intended more for the benefit of his "guest" than her. She glanced nervously at the man she assumed to be Jerardo Capella. He was short and wiry with a thick slick of white hair that was muted to a greasy battleship gray with strong hair product. A small mouth parted to send her a nicotine stained leer, his attempt at a smile. His eyes were masked by ostentatiously large sunglasses, but she'd bet his gaze was cold and nasty behind them. How did Ricardo get involved with this unsavory character? She'd assumed the bet was with one of his young playboy contemporaries, all flashy cars and fast women, not an older man like this. But what did she know? Ricardo was no ordinary man and Jerardo Capella might be a perfectly pleasant individual...

The ceremony was quick and few words were spoken. The registrar clearly had time to make up in his busy schedule that morning, and the way Ricardo had bitten out his responses made it obvious that he wanted to get out of the place as quickly as possible. The civil wedding vows were basic and business-like. Their duties and rights as a married couple were set out: family, fidelity, and management of the home, and children's education. Not once was the word love mentioned, so at least Ricardo was in the clear there. There was no "until death us do part" nonsense, so the whole "celebration" was as contractual as their secret agreement.

The registrar pronounced them husband and wife, wiping beads of sweat from his brow with undisguised relief and Ricardo's perfunctory kiss on Helen's cheek left her with a choking sense of humiliation. What had she expected? That Ricardo had fallen head over heels in love with her overnight? That a miracle had occurred and that all this was for real? As if.

Helen was cross with herself for weakening the moment she'd seen him that morning. The black suit and arctic white shirt had given him such an astonishing presence that she could almost feel her bones dissolve under his scrutiny. The strong black eyebrows that were knitted together with irritation made her want to reach out and stroke his temple until he smiled, took her in his arms and kissed her. He was dark, menacing and angry, but in spite of all that, she still wanted him.

She still wanted him even though he had left her side within seconds, not without even a backwards glance. It had been deeply embarrassing, standing there in front of two awkward-looking officials while Ricardo and Jerardo put their arrogant heads together. Where was her pride? She felt as if she'd been dumped already.

Luisa patted Helen's hand as she stared stonily towards Ricardo and Jerardo exchanging documents. "He is nervous today, you must understand." Her tiny brown eyes twinkled anxiously, the atmosphere in the room was tense, hardly one of celebration and joy. It didn't take a genius to work out that something wasn't quite right.

"Why is Jerardo Capella here?" Luisa murmured. "Are you friends?"

Helen shrugged and looked at the floor. She felt unable to lie much longer so it would be better to say nothing.

Luisa fussed with Helen's hair. "He always brings bad luck that one. I could have brought my brother if you needed another witness to the marriage."

Helen took an angry breath. "Actually, I'd like to know

what he's doing here as well." She stalked purposefully towards the two men, who looked up in surprise from the papers they were signing. She held out her hand and shot the stranger a tight smile. "I don't think you've introduced me to your friend, Ricardo."

"He's an uncivilized dog, isn't he?" the stranger replied greasily, and straightened his back. "Jerardo Capella at your service. We go back a long way, Ricardo and I. When he's grown tired of you, come round to my place and I'll show you how a real Spanish man treats a beautiful woman."

"*Basta!* Enough!" Ricardo bellowed, snapping the lid on his pen and throwing it onto the table. "It's time you left now, Capella. You have an office to clear out, remember?"

"So true, I almost forgot in my excitement." Jerardo slid past the desk and snatched at Helen's hand. His breath was hot, and the sweaty kiss he planted lasted a lot longer than it should have. Revulsion coiled in Helen's stomach.

"Get out," Ricardo said. "Before I damage you."

"How does it feel to be traded for a derelict building, Senora Almanza?" He smiled at her confusion and went in for the kill. "He should value your beauty much more highly. You have no idea how much it costs every year to scrape off all the pigeon shit and dog mess from the place…"

"I think maybe you should do as Ricardo says and leave," Helen said flatly. She didn't want the creep to see how deeply he was offending her.

"I'm not surprised he didn't tell you. It's not very flattering for you, is it?" He whipped off his sunglasses, and the black eyes that bored into hers *were* cruel. "Oh dear, he didn't tell you he *loved* you did he? Now that really was unkind…"

Helen bit down hard on her bottom lip as the sparking pain of tears attacked the back of her throat.

No, of course he'd never said he loved her. He'd been

decent about that.

Rage blazed in Ricardo's eyes as he roughly shoved Jerardo away and pulled Helen protectively against him, his arm tight around her waist. "You'll never get anywhere near what we have together. Now get out, and if I ever discover you've been near my wife again I'll kill you."

Jerardo sneered and put his shades back on with a shrug. "It'll never last, Almanza. You're cursed."

Helen flinched as he slammed the door behind him and the sound echoed around the walls like a round of cannon fire. *What we have together?* The words stuck like a fiery brand on her mind, poised to give her false hope.

•

"I'm sorry you had to go through that," Ricardo said in a matter of fact way as the limousine drove them both away.

"Jerardo Capella, you mean?" Helen said smartly. "Or the whole charade?"

"You know exactly what I mean. There was no need for such unpleasantness. I had tried to dissuade him from attending but," he sighed heavily, "he's not a reasonable man."

Helen braced herself. She had to clarify what Ricardo had said earlier. "What did you mean when you spoke to Jerardo about what 'we had together'?"

Ricardo looked at her incredulously. "Sexual chemistry, of course. What else could I have been alluding to? The extremely devious arrangement we came to purely for exacting revenge on that snake?" He shook his head and smiled. "You don't think I'd risk letting him in on our deal, do you?"

"I have no idea what you're capable of."

"I've gone to extreme lengths to get back what rightfully belongs to the Almanza family, so I don't intend risking it all by letting Capella discover our marriage is a sham. Although, I think he was too busy lusting over you to be thinking particularly clearly. He never was the brightest, just downright nasty." Ricardo grinned and did a little whistle, oblivious to the sharp disappointment that had sliced right through her at his words.

"So you got everything you wanted?" she said, staring out at the busy marketplace through the smoked glass of the car window.

"Not everything, Senora Almanza, not yet…" He shot her a look so charged with sexual promise that it took Helen's breath away.

"Honor intact now?" She wasn't going to let him see how much she was hurting, or how bizarrely her heart was pounding at the prospect of their wedding night in spite of his coldness.

"Oh *that*," he said, threading his fingers through hers and lifting their linked hands to inspect the two rings on her left. "Yes."

"Care to expand on that? Just how much do derelict, poo-covered buildings go for in this part of the world?" She tugged her hand away. "For more than two million presumably or all of this would be pointless."

"You weren't traded, Helen. Far from it. The deal was for the *right* to buy the building, not to walk off with the deeds as soon as I married. I had to pay a significant amount more to make it legally mine, believe me. And it's going to need to be completely gutted."

"Am I being dim here? Let me get this clear. You won the bet by getting married before you were thirty, right?"

"Correct."

"So what did you actually win? An *option* to purchase?

"Correct."

Helen felt slightly dumbfounded. "So what if you lost the bet and forgot all about the crumbling pile of real estate. That way you wouldn't have had to go through with this grotesque marriage or waste all that money. Or is this really a matter of your stupid, arrogant pride?"

"Incorrect. To lose Capella's bet would have meant me breaking the promise I made to my father on his deathbed, a promise to reclaim the Almanza Imperial Department Store and restore the family's honor. It was stolen from us effectively via a series of unethical legal maneuvers when my father was…indisposed. In the last ten years Capella has let the building go to the dogs, literally when it comes to the outside of it, and he's a hopeless businessman. The staff he retained from the old days was given their cards this month, the stock has gone, and it's all in a real mess. It is my duty to do my best to get it up and running again, not only for future Almanzas, but for the poor people who were such loyal employees. I could never forgive myself if I didn't give it my best shot. So I had no choice but to give in to Capella's conditions."

"This wasn't really a bet after all, was it? You let me think you were a shallow, spendthrift playboy who'd made one stupid drunken bet to marry. Why didn't you tell me the truth from the start?" Helen blinked her eyes with indignation. "Capella is a disgusting little blackmailer."

"I can think of more appropriate descriptions, but I wouldn't want to defile those beautiful, innocent ears of yours," Ricardo said with a smile. "And as for the truth about why I needed a bride, would it have made any difference to your answer? You only agreed to my conditions when you were totally desperate for the money. You walked out on me in disgust when I first made the offer in Ibiza, didn't you? Your principles were so high, no way would you be bought, for whatever reason…"

Helen felt her cheeks flush and she lowered her head in the hope that he wouldn't notice. "I don't need to listen to this—"

"But two million easy euros was too much for you to resist, wasn't it, darling?" Ricardo picked up her hands again and kissed the tips of her fingers one by one. "And now everyone's happy. Capella has his cash and the satisfaction of believing I am miserably married. You have your second million in the bank as of midday, and—" He leaned back into the soft leather of the seat and slowly stroked the palm of her hand with his forefinger. "Now it's *my* turn to get some reward for all this. Let me tell you, Helen Almanza, I am really, *really* looking forward to our honeymoon. In fact…" He took her chin firmly between his fingers and turned her face up towards him. His hovered just inches from hers. "I see no reason why we shouldn't make a start right now."

Chapter Six

"We shouldn't…not here," Helen said in a light, shaky voice as his fingers pulled out a hairpin at the nape of her neck. "Not in the back of a car with the driver inches away."

"We're newlyweds and should do whatever we like," he murmured before pulling her into an intense kiss.

He silently extracted the remaining pins and she felt her hair tumble free over her jaw and shoulders as he eased her head back into the soft leather of the car seat. Helen clung to the fine fabric of his suit and quivered as his tongue entered her mouth and she matched him stroke for stroke as the kiss deepened. Their first kiss on the Condesa's terrace hadn't felt like this. That kiss, the one that sealed their immoral marriage deal, had felt more like a punishment, a warning, a proprietary branding. It had been hard and fierce, but she'd gone up in flames of lust for him even then. This time was different. This time she was melting. She was melting into his blistering kisses, helpless, like an ice cube on hot sand.

Helen was more than a willing participant. She was now his wife, to have and to hold. And to kiss and to…have sex with for three months. She was lost to his touch and she wanted him to take her more than was sane. The Condesa was right. He would show her the ecstasy of his bed, fill her, empty her, and then destroy her. And she would let him, because there was no way she could resist the way he made her body feel. Her fate was decided.

His mouth drifted to her neck and she arched with pleasure, her eyes opening as she did so. "Where are we going?" she suddenly asked, blinking to restore her vision. The street they were driving through seemed unfamiliar.

"Our honeymoon," Ricardo whispered against the soft skin over her collarbone and began to stroke her thigh beneath the hem of her wedding dress. "We just got married, remember?"

Her body stiffened as his hand went higher. "But this isn't the way we came yesterday, and all the road signs to Marbella are pointing the wrong way."

"Relax. We're not going to Marbella."

A lance of panic sliced through her. She didn't like being completely out of control of a situation. She was coming to her senses. "Tell me where we're going immediately," she replied sharply. "Or—"

"Or you'll scream? Call the police? Again? Honestly…" His tone was exasperated as he pulled back and stared at her. "You'll notice that we are about to enter the harbor. The exclusive berth where my yacht is docked lies beyond that red and white barrier. Once we're on board, you can go anywhere you like. She can go five thousand miles without refueling."

"Oh…"

"Problem?"

"*Mal de mer.*"

"What?"

Her stomach churned. "It doesn't matter, but…" She dropped her bouquet onto the floor of the car. "I think I'm going to be sick."

"You're joking, right?" Ricardo laughed awkwardly.

Helen looked up with panic into his incredulous face and felt indignant fury as he did absolutely nothing. "Stop the bloody car," she gasped. "I'm going to be really ill!"

Finally realizing that she was serious, Ricardo rapped on the glass partition to get the driver to pull over. Wrenching open the car door, Helen tumbled out and lurched towards the quayside. The sea breeze was strong as it cut across the harbor, but nothing was going to quell the urgent nausea she was experiencing. She threw up within seconds. Between acrid retches, she touched her clammy forehead with shaking fingers. She was aware that Ricardo's large hand brushed against her, hesitantly at first, then more confidently, rubbing comforting circles between her shoulder blades. He held out a snow-white handkerchief and put it under her nose as she convulsed towards the sea again.

"I do hope there's no one down there," he said lightly. "Or they're going to get quite an unpleasant shock when your breakfast hits them."

"Don't be a disgusting pig, Ricardo," Helen said between retches. She was reminding herself of a cat with fur balls, most unladylike. This really was the ultimate indignity.

"Care to tell me what's going on?" Ricardo said when Helen finally managed to stand upright. "I can't believe the thought of being my wife is *that* abhorrent. Or do I really kiss that badly? You seem to have a daily episode of fainting or general wimpishness lately." He gripped her shoulders and forced her to look him in the eye. "*Dios!* You've not turned to the bottle, have you? Bellinis for breakfast?" He made a point of sniffing suspiciously at her mouth.

"Don't be ridiculous!" Helen said, shrugging her shoulders angrily out of his grip. "If you must know, I've not been feeling quite right since we came back from England. I keep waking up with headaches, and I've had quite a few episodes of feeling sickly, but none as bad as today." She brushed a stray lock of hair from her face and inhaled the cool fresh air slowly. "It's probably stress and the change of environment. I didn't have much breakfast either, so it could be that." She was quick to add, "not that Luisa didn't do her best. She ordered up enough food for a week."

Ricardo took her pale face in his large brown hands. He studied her inquisitively for a moment or two. She was so tiny and delicate, like a seed pearl shining underwater, beautiful yet surprisingly resilient under pressure. He felt an unfamiliar lurch in the pit of his stomach, a twist of something he didn't understand, and it unsettled him.

"This is all my fault. I've driven you too hard, not noticed you were ill in my impatience to get today out of the way." His expression was grim as he pulled her head to rest on the crisp white of his wedding shirt. "Let's get you back in the car. We've not far to go and then you can rest. You need to be taken care of."

"I'm not sure taking me onto your boat is going to help matters. I was as sick as a dog for a week after my uncle took me mackerel fishing. I've not been on the water since."

"*Indalo* is no trawler," he muttered. "You'll be fine."

. . .

Doctor Romano looked at Ricardo sternly. "I've left her to rest now and told her that in no circumstances must she start taking those pills again. In fact, I've removed the supply she was prescribed in case she's tempted." He tossed the foil sachets into his black case and snapped it shut. "I know how these independent career women can be about such things, trying their best to control nature and events, but in this instance the medication is making your wife ill. It's uncommon, but the contraceptive pill just doesn't suit some women."

"I knew she should have consulted a decent private physician, not some tourist quack."

The doctor shrugged and picked up his bag. "Anyway, you're married now, so it's not something any self-respecting Almanza needs to worry about." He regarded Ricardo mischievously over the horn rims of his spectacles. "So when the Senora is feeling better, enjoy your honeymoon, and give me a call when her period's late."

As the cabin door closed quietly behind him, Ricardo's fists clenched and his thoughts began to trip over each other in the rush. Subconsciously, the back of his hand flew to his mouth, as if to stifle a roar of anger. His lips made contact with the cool metal of his wedding band and crushing guilt smothered him.

He was a beast. His pride and lust had cajoled her into a situation she didn't want. He had behaved in a disgusting manner and was now feeling wretched with self-loathing. He could imagine the contempt Doctor Romano would have for him if he knew it was his big, clever idea to persuade Helen to go on the pill or similar, to satisfy his urgent physical longing for the woman without risk of repercussion. He shuddered as he imagined the old family physician's reaction. You simply didn't treat a woman like that.

But she'd gone along with the marriage, hadn't she? She had agreed to *that* in exchange for his money? So, okay, maybe he shouldn't feel bad about that side of things. But the sex? She had made it quite clear that she wasn't going into his bed because she wanted to and that was something he *could* fix. The last thing he really wanted, apart from marriage, was to force himself on an unwilling woman. That was the sort of thing Jerardo would do, and he really *was* disgusting. Why on earth hadn't he realized how he'd been behaving before now? If his brother Primeiro had been around he would have spoken his mind, told him to get a grip and treat the woman with some respect. *Dios!* He missed his brother…

· · ·

Helen awoke and was alarmed to see Ricardo tiptoeing into her room with a tray. "How long have I been asleep?" she asked, propping herself up on one elbow.

"Shh!" He took her hand firmly in his and kissed it affectionately. "You needed to rest."

"How sweet." Helen was taken aback by his sudden concern and gentleness. "You bringing me tea is very kind."

"The least I could do."

Helen took a sip, then put the cup thoughtfully back down into its saucer and summoned the courage to tell him what the doctor had said earlier. "Listen, Ricardo. I have to speak to you about what the doctor said—"

Ricardo silenced her with a finger pad to her lips. "It's fine, I know all about it." He sighed apologetically. "I'm afraid there's no such thing as patient confidentiality when you're married to an Almanza. But here." He took a bundle of papers from the bedside table. "I have something for you. A wedding gift."

"Oh no! Not more agreements to sign!" Helen's voice rose in anguish. No wonder he was being so sweet, he was going in for the kill again! "I know things aren't going quite like you planned, but I'm sure we can straighten them out, seek a second opinion or something!"

"*Basta!* Enough." Ricardo blasted with agitation and then appeared to regret it as Helen shrank away from him.

He coughed. "Sorry, I didn't mean to shout. These are the documents we signed originally, and there is something I feel you should be aware of." He spoke more softly now. "I'm sure you didn't read them all through, and not having a lawyer's understanding of matters it may not have made much difference if you had. What I'm trying to tell you is that nowhere in this mass of paper does it mention any marital duties."

"It doesn't? But—"

"It would probably be breaking the law to make such a contract, anyway. That part of the deal was just between you and me." He placed the papers back on the table and walked slowly towards the door. "So, I'm releasing you from that side of the bargain. The money is yours to keep and you are under no legal or moral obligation to sleep with me. I do hope you like your wedding present, Helen." He looked thoughtfully out towards the sound of crashing waves outside. "And in no time I'll give you your name back too."

As the cabin door shut behind him, Helen suppressed the urge to yell "don't I have any say in any of this?" but the words dried in her mouth as she struggled to absorb what had happened since they'd boarded the yacht. She was off the pill and Ricardo? Ricardo was suddenly *off* her! She had been unceremoniously dumped from his bedroom plans. So did this mean he'd now be straight off to some high-class bordello to satisfy his *marital* needs? He'd have to "protect" himself there presumably. Or maybe not. She had no idea how these things worked, but she was suddenly feeling a lot healthier. She was suddenly feeling extremely angry too.

"Now you come back here!" she yelled, storming out on deck with just a silk robe over her underwear. "We still have things to talk about, Ricardo Almanza. Don't you dare dismiss me."

Ricardo leaned against the glass balcony overlooking the ocean, and his bronze eyes widened in astonishment. "Please don't let me stop you in full flow," he said politely and gestured for her to sit on one of the luxurious sun loungers laid out for them. "Talk away."

"Well," Helen said, the thunder having been well and truly stolen from her. "I want to know what happens from here. Do I sit around and play the dutiful wife for three months while you cavort with the nearest supermodel? Part of our convenient marriage vows did deal with the subject of fidelity, as you may recall. I know the whole thing is as sham, but I don't think I could stand being totally humiliated."

"Not even for all that money?" Ricardo said quietly, his forefinger pressed against his temple.

"No. I do have some self-respect." Helen squeezed her lips together in a desperate attempt to stop the angry irrational tears she could feel welling up.

Ricardo sighed and rubbed his eyes laboriously with the heels of his hands. "*Dios!* I thought I was making things easier for you. Why aren't you happy now?"

"Because—because…" She searched for a plausible reason. "You said you wanted me."

Ricardo let out a shaky laugh and lightly scratched the darkening shadow that was beginning to appear on his square jaw. "That hasn't changed."

"Then I don't understand. What *has* changed since we got back here?"

"I've had time to think in the last twenty-four hours. I came to the conclusion that this is exactly the sort of situation where I have to accept the word no. I should have done so in the very beginning. Our marriage is a legitimate contract between us and is valid in the eyes of the law. However, the other matter, the physical side of our deal, well, that's something that should never be taken or paid for." He formed a tent shape with his fingers and balanced his chin on it lightly. "It should always be a gift, and for that I'm sorry." He shrugged and averted his eyes for a second. "I wanted you in my bed so much that I got carried away, forgot that this was all about my family honor in the first place. Too much testosterone. Too much temptation within my reach."

"Like with the car?"

Ricardo leaned back and clasped his hands behind his neck, ignorant to the astonishing display his biceps were giving by doing so. "Should I compare thee to a red Ferrari?"

Helen felt her face crack into an involuntary smile. "You are such a smooth, spoiled git, Almanza…"

He gestured a silent 'of course' with his a flourish of his long hands and gave her a smile so devastating in its sexual pull that she had to take a sharp intake of breath.

"So what next?" Ricardo said slowly.

"I don't know," she said, thinking that this now sounded a bit like discussing a restaurant menu. "What do you suggest?"

"We have a fully-stocked yacht, staff, and a quarter of a million dollar's worth of fuel on board. I have land and property just about everywhere in the Mediterranean and North Africa. There's a helicopter and a speedboat tucked away somewhere on this vessel." He teased her with a long pause. "So we could always throw caution to the wind and enjoy our honeymoon."

"Our honeymoon…"

He held up his hands in a gesture of surrender. "No strings. No expectations. Just a holiday. But we have to be realistic. It's only a matter of time before the paparazzi get wind of where we are every time we make land. Our wedding and honeymoon pictures will be changing hands for a lot of money until another big story comes along. Malaga and

Ibiza will be a nightmare, but they'll have trouble getting to us in Menorca. We can get some peace there." He leaned back against the balcony railing, his face easing into one of *those* smiles again. "So what do you think of this idea? We cooperate with the press, give the pack some good shots of us together in Ibiza, some quotes even, on the understanding they give us some privacy afterwards."

"Do you think they will?"

"No. But if the payoff for exclusive shots drops we won't be quite a tempting mark. "

"It does seem like a good idea."

"And I expect you're missing the party scene already."

"Well, not exactly."

He shot her a disbelieving look. "So all we need to decide now is how quickly we get there. If we stay cruising at this speed we should make Ibiza by morning. Alternatively, we can take the helicopter to Malaga right now, transfer to my private jet, and it will take us less than three hours."

Helen did her best not to let her eyes grow as large as saucers. "We'd be there in time for dinner."

He smiled. "We'd be there before the clubs in San Antonio even wake up."

"Money is bloody useful sometimes."

"It is."

She despised herself for the way looking at him made her feel. His dark hair lifted and fell in the breeze, and the way he could stare at her for moments at a time without flinching set her blood on fire. Helen wished the distance between them wasn't so wide so she could feel his breath on her skin. She wished he would roll down the crisp white silk of his shirt to hide the corded muscles of his tanned forearms. She wished she could stop her heart dancing the tarantella in her chest.

She wished he would take her to bed.

They needed to get off the yacht fast before she did something she'd regret.

"Yes," she whispered. "Yes, let's do it."

•

The huge diamond on Helen's ring finger flashed as she ran her hand film-star style through her hair and the paparazzi cameras lit up the night sky. She was showing off like a natural on the parapets of Ibiza town and looked stunning in the red silk wrap dress she'd chosen from her trousseau. She had conspired in his tipping off the biggest news agencies before they'd arrived, seemed quite excited by the prospect and was now acting up a storm.

To Ricardo's surprise Helen was turning out to be the perfect media wife if her current performance was anything to go by.

"Why Ibiza for your wedding night, Ricardo?" a paparazzi shouted.

"Why not?" he called back. "It's where we met, the White Isle, and we love it here."

A female photographer leaned in close, the tool of her trade still clicking like a cicada. "Going clubbing later?"

Ricardo blinked in the flashlights, but smiled graciously. "Of course."

The woman switched her attention to Helen. "Mrs. Almanza, what's it like to be married to the ex—most eligible man in Europe?"

"Just Europe?" Helen grinned. "It's wonderful. Ricardo is the man of my dreams, perfect in every way…"

There was a ripple of applause and the sea of flashing cameras acted like a lightning storm.

"Guys." Ricardo gestured with his hands that the mob

should settle. "It's deal time. We give you an exclusive if you let us have an evening meal in peace. It *is* our honeymoon after all." There was a collective affirmative murmur and a few wolf whistles. "I guess that's a yes. Okay."

Ricardo's ears rang with the roar of the crowd as he took Helen in his arms and kissed her hard. She arched her body into his, running her hands through his hair and he felt a burst of shock as she raised her thigh to wrap it around his hip. The skirt of her wrap dress fell open and he hurriedly grasped her leg in an attempt to cover her bare flesh, but the way her tongue was behaving in his mouth told him modesty was not at the forefront of her mind. Her being crushed so wantonly against him exacerbated the involuntary stiffening below his belt. They were in danger of making a worldwide spectacle of themselves. He pulled his mouth away and eased her leg back down to the ground. "Easy," he whispered harshly into her hair. "You've given them enough."

"And I was having so much fun," she whispered back.

His tone was stern. "Later."

The crowd parted as Ricardo painted on a billionaire playboy smile, and his security team cleared their path to an exclusive restaurant entrance nearby. He didn't enjoy having to be a performing seal, but sometimes it was unavoidable. However, the last thing he needed was a loose cannon for a wife for the next three months making things even worse. A performance like that would guarantee even more interest in them. He could see the rash of vulgar magazine covers already, with her smooth pale thigh taking centre stage. He suppressed a shiver and was relieved to reach the sanctuary of a private restaurant balcony overlooking Ibiza harbor.

Ricardo ordered champagne and then waited in silence until the restaurant owner left them alone with the menus. "You didn't need to go quite so far out there."

"No? It's what they wanted, what you wanted. We should get some peace now. You said we would."

"That performance has probably made matters worse. The pictures will go worldwide by morning, and the entire planet's press will be drooling over what Senora Almanza is going to do next." He picked up a knife and tapped the handle rhythmically on the table. "And what will your parents think?"

"They don't buy newspapers or any magazine besides *Farmers Weekly*. I shouldn't think they'll notice."

"It will be all over the Internet."

Helen chuckled. "They don't have a computer or watch anything other than local TV and *that* gets switched off after the local news." She twirled her wine glass between her fingers and watched the bubbles dance for a few seconds. "Besides, they think we're besotted newlyweds, for God's sake. Where's the problem?"

There was no problem. The problem was all inside him and the way he had felt when she had flaunted herself that way. The tension knotting his neck and shoulders was a strong as a trawler's net. "Your bra is showing."

Helen glanced down at the tiny glimpse of black satin and lace that was peeking out underneath the red silk of her dress. "It's supposed to show. It's the fashion with this sort of neckline."

"Really?"

"Oh come on, Ricardo, let's cut out all the prudery. Playboy billionaires don't date shrinking violets, do they? Let alone marry one."

"You surprised me, that's all. I didn't think you were like that."

"Like what?"

"Exuberant."

She bent to whisper across the table. "Of course you didn't. You don't know me at all. It's a marriage of convenience, remember? A marriage to win a bet."

"To settle a matter of honor."

"Oh yes, of course, silly me."

"A marriage for which you've been well paid. Please don't forget that in all your excitement."

Chapter Seven

"Had enough?"

Helen nodded and didn't even try to shout her reply to Ricardo over the pounding music and fireworks inside the club. She was soaked to the skin with sweat and sickly sweet smelling alcohol, and although he'd bought her plenty of water to drink, the dry ice and unbearable heat made her throat feel like sandpaper. Her chest was feeling tighter by the minute. He had taken her to three of the most famous clubs in Ibiza, hotly pursued by photographers. As far as her love of clubbing was concerned he had well and truly called her bluff.

She slipped off her scarlet heels and dangled them from her fingertips as a bouncer led them through a "Staff Only" door. As it closed behind them, the throb of the music still vibrated under her bare feet and her ears were muzzy, but at least she now felt better able to breathe again. She shot Ricardo a look over her shoulder. "I don't want to have to do that again in a hurry!"

Ricardo, following close behind, was disarmingly disheveled. "No need to shout," he mouthed playfully.

Helen grinned back. "Sorry, deaf as a post, so noisy in there!"

The air outside the back door of the club was cool on her face and the sky shimmered with stars as Ricardo relieved her of her handbag and then took her by the hand as they walked down a side street towards the marina. "I thought you'd want to stay for a few more hours."

The palm of his hand was dry and warm, wrapped around hers and she fought the urge to squeeze it. "Perhaps now would be the time to confess that I've never been that into the clubbing scene."

"Seriously?"

"Tonight was my second time and how can you be surprised? I asked someone how much it cost to get in when you were in the loo. A hundred euros one bloke paid and that's before you start spending fifteen euros on a drink!"

"You know money's not a problem now."

"And I don't like the music that much either."

Ricardo chuckled and surprised her by suddenly stopping in the middle of the deserted street. He pulled her into his chest until his mouth was inches from hers. "Thank God for that," he muttered and kissed her softly on the lips.

Helen's eyes closed and she didn't resist as the kiss deepened. Couldn't resist. His mouth felt and tasted too good. Her nerve endings sizzled as his warm fingers trailed the length of her neck, skimmed the sides of her breasts and then closed around her waist, pulling her tightly against him in the cool night air. She wasn't doing a very good job of pretending she didn't want him, but was too tired to fight it anymore. "We should find somewhere to sleep," she whispered as his mouth found the pulse in her neck. "There's always my place. I've a spare key hidden outside still."

"I'm never letting you go back to that dump." He brushed

his fingers across her breast, lingering on the tight bead that was pushing against the silk of her dress. "However much I want to take advantage of you right now."

"We could—"

"I own the Gran Finca Hotel, woman. And the Playa Caribe." He laughed into her hair. "That equates to at least a hundred king size beds with air conditioning and breakfast in the morning."

"Oh."

"But I'm feeling wild now the fresh air's hit me. I want to take you down to the beach and—"

"Hey!"

Helen jumped at the sound of another man's voice behind them. It was familiar.

"Helen! Marshymallow! It's me!"

She turned to see a man in cut off jeans with shoulder-length blond hair and tattooed arms. "Bjorn!"

"It is you! I'd recognize that arse anywhere. Nice dress!"

Ricardo's arms tightened around her waist. She smiled back cheerfully at the other man. "Thank you."

"Would you care to introduce me to your... friend?"

"Oh, yes, sorry. Ricardo, this is Bjorn. We worked together once and he runs the archaeology course I went to before, before you and I met." She held her breath as Bjorn held out his hand. Ricardo didn't return the gesture for a few seconds. To her relief he eventually did. "And Bjorn, Ricardo is my very new husband."

Bjorn's sandy-colored eyebrows snapped together over his blue eyes. "Husband! But it was only two weeks ago we—"

"It's been a bit of a whirlwind romance. I've not had a chance to tell everyone yet."

"Well." Bjorn raked nail-bitten fingers through his mane and appeared to force a smile. "I guess it's congratulations to you guys. Want to come back to mine for a bite to eat? We could crack open a few beers, watch the sun rise with one of my signature curries."

"Oh that's very kind of you, but—"

"But we need to be somewhere," Ricardo said abruptly.

Bjorn sighed. "Finishing your sentences for each other already?" His smile faded. "How cute."

Ricardo glared back. "And we're running late."

"I get the message, big guy," Bjorn said cockily, and reached out to run a fingertip over Helen's shoulder. "You know where I am if, well, y'know…"

Helen felt Ricardo's tension make her own body stiffen. "Everything's fine," she said firmly. "See you around."

"You *won't*," Ricardo muttered as they watched him stride off down an alleyway. "Not if I have anything to do with it anyway."

"You don't own me, Almanza."

"You're my wife and we have a business deal. Associating with people like that is beneath someone of your standing now."

"What?"

Ricardo ignored the disbelief that must have been obvious on her face. "If you want beer and curry I will buy it for you, you don't need that hippy."

"Are you a tiny bit drunk?"

Ricardo sniffed and looked around them for a moment. "A little. We were having a good time before he turned up."

"Then stop sulking." She giggled at his jealous outburst. "Buy me a kebab from somewhere, will you. I'm starving!"

• • •

Ricardo watched as Helen wrapped both her hands around

a meat-stuffed pita bread and sank her teeth hungrily into it. He'd never seen a woman do anything like that before. Food had always been a neat and tidy, finger-picking, delicate-morsel-nibbling affair. She was fascinating. She was so completely different from any female he had ever known. He looked down at his own extra large gyro and took the plunge.

"You've got sauce on your chin," she mumbled after swallowing a mouthful. She reached across to wipe it off with the tip of her finger. "And you could do with a shave."

"Thanks. And this is an experience," he said as he peered into the bread-wrapped tangle of salad and chilies.

Her bare feet dangled like a child's over the harbor's edge where they'd settled to eat. "It's like a different world down here in the dark. I can hardly hear the clubs and crowds now."

"Hmm." Ricardo tugged at a long thread of onion and grimaced. "Security won't let the rabble into the marina, people like dodgy Bjorn. Berth holders only."

"You took an instant dislike to him, didn't you?" She offered him a pickled chili, but he wrinkled his nose with disgust. "Anyone would think you were jealous. As well as being an abysmal snob."

"I bet he takes drugs," Ricardo said, unfazed as he stared out to sea.

"Oh honestly…"

"Did you sleep with him?"

"What?"

"You heard."

"None of your business."

"I'm your husband, so it's definitely my business."

"You're my sham husband, don't forget." She twisted the paper kebab wrapper. "But for what it's worth we're just friends. No sex, just good times and digging for broken pottery."

"He wants to sleep with you."

Her laughter tinkled in the night air. "That's not going to happen."

"Good."

"That's not going to happen with *anyone* right now."

"Half an hour ago things were different. As I recall, Mrs. Almanza, you were on the verge of dragging me off to your student flat to make love amongst the cockroaches."

"I was not!" She laughed again and her cheeks flushed pink in the blue-white light of the moon.

"Liar," he said and handed her the crumpled remains of his kebab. "Want to finish this?"

"Is that supposed to be a love offering? Caveman style. Me feed you, me take you back to me, um, cave?"

She really was intriguing. Unpredictable. "If you want it to be." His voice was soft as he took her by the hand and kissed her salty fingertips. "Garlic and mint. You are a divine creature." She giggled and he felt a wave of pleasure wash over him.

"I'm tempted," she said quietly and his stomach flipped as she stared up at him with serious green eyes. "Tempted to say yes, but—"

"But what?"

"It would complicate things between us."

"It needn't. Just wild, consensual sex between sham husband and sham wife. No strings." He shrugged as if it was unimportant to him. "We're attracted to each other and both grown ups, not star-crossed teenagers who'll fall madly in love or anything."

Her eyes sparkled like the tiny dark waves lapping at the sea wall. "Or bunny boilers."

He laughed softly and poked the top of her arm playfully. "It's a serious proposition. Three months fulfilling your wildest fantasies. With me."

"You're mad."

"You're considering it, I can tell."

"I'm not!"

"Ah! Perfect timing." He pointed towards the harbor mouth as a pyramid of lights came into view. His yacht was floating in like a ghostly galleon. "I'll tell the captain to turn straight round and take us to Menorca."

"Poor crew! Can't they even stop off for a beer or something?"

"They won't mind. I pay them a ridiculous amount to stay sober."

"But even so…"

"There are two shifts of men on board, don't worry. I'm not *that* bad!"

•

Helen was shattered, but try as she might sleep would not come. It wasn't the low hum of the yacht's engines keeping her awake. Its soothing purr was barely audible. And the crew were as quiet as mice. In fact, it was so peaceful that she could hear the splash and hiss of waves hitting the bows outside. She should be fast asleep after the hectic day she'd had, but the gentle rise and fall of the yacht, as it made its way across the Mediterranean ocean towards the island of Menorca, was provoking feelings she shouldn't be having.

Ricardo had kissed her goodnight before disappearing into his own cabin. It had been a deep kiss as opposed to a polite one, and she was sorry when it ended. A small part of her had hoped he'd sweep her off her feet and drag her into his bed to finish what they'd started on the dark back streets of Ibiza. The swell of the waves made her imagine what it would be like to be underneath him as he moved rhythmically over and into her under the cover of night, and it was driving her insane.She rolled over and buried her face in a pillow to stifle the groan of frustration that she could no longer suppress. She wanted him. He wanted her. All the cards were face up on the table. His three-month proposition. Lying there with her breasts crushed into the mattress she knew it was her turn to make a move. He wasn't going to come and fetch her, he'd said as much as he'd left her to go to bed alone. It was her choice and his adjoining cabin door would be unlocked…

Damn it.

Helen turned the doorknob as quietly as she could, acknowledging inwardly that it was a pointless thing to do. She wasn't intending for Ricardo to ignore her. Her intention was so shocking she smothered the thought and all reason with it as she pushed the door to his suite open.

Her skin tingled beneath the whisper of her silk robe, and she could feel her nipples tighten the second she stepped into his bedroom. It was dark and silent, but as her eyes adjusted to the light it became clear that his enormous bed was empty— it hadn't even been slept in judging by the smooth order of the bed linen. Her breath stalled as she saw him silhouetted against the night sky, framed by the open glass doors that led onto the terrace, his private part of the deck that wasn't overlooked by anyone.

He was leaning to one side with his back to her, his broad shoulder against one side of the doorframe, his upper body a perfectly honed triangle of muscle and bone. She took one step forward, but as her bare foot sank into the luxurious carpet his voice made her stop dead. "You came."

Her tone was deceptively calm. "Yes." She could now see that he was naked, and her hand shook as she untied the belt of her robe. The fine material slithered to the floor as she walked towards him. "Would you like me to leave?"

He turned to face her in the shadows, moonlight glimmering on the smooth angles of his shoulders. "What do you want, Helen?"

Could he see where she was looking? He was perfect. He was huge. Her reply was hoarse as she laid the palm of her hand on his chest. "I want my husband." She trailed her fingertips down over his stomach and felt his hands grip her bare shoulders as she dropped to her knees in front of him.

"You don't have to—"

"I said I wanted my husband," she whispered and cautiously stroked the length of him with her fingertips in the darkness. "Let me."

He groaned as she took him into the soft heat of her mouth and savored the way he felt. Ridged hot velvet over steel, but too much to take him all the way in. Her lips slowly slid back and forth, dragging his foreskin with a teasing motion that made his thigh muscles twitch. It thrilled her to feel him beginning to lose control under her touch. It gave her power over him.

His large hands cupped both her breasts before slowly running his thumb pads over her tight nipples. His breathing was becoming heavier. "You witch."

"*Whore*," she whispered and pushed his length between her breasts. Saying the word excited her. It liberated her. She was living a lie and could be anyone now. She was enjoying this game, and the way his penis strained between them told her he was ready to play too. "You paid for me, remember?" She rolled the tip of her tongue over the head of his erection, dipping into the tender slit at the end, and gripped him gently between the legs to provoke him beyond endurance.

Ignoring her small cry of surprise, he swung her up from the floor and dropped her heavily down onto the bed.

His knee was between her legs and easing her thighs apart before she could catch her breath. "You want your husband to make love to you? Is that what you're trying to make me do?" His mouth crushed her response, but she lifted her legs and rubbed her damp sex against him so there could be no mistake as to what she wanted.

He pulled his mouth away from hers and trailed his tongue down her throat, between her breasts, and then around the areole of her nipple. "I want you to have me any way you like," she muttered and pushed his mouth down and around the stiff peak of her breast. "But hard. And soon."

She gasped as his forefinger found her entrance, slicked her clitoris with her own juices and then slid inside. A second finger followed, slid, flicked and pushed her apart until she felt a third join them. His voice was unsteady as his thumb applied pressure to the sensitive rise of her mound and began to move in slow circles. "You like?"

"I like." She moaned and reached down between them to grasp his erection. It was huge and hot, his foreskin fully drawn back in anticipation, its wide head swollen and ready. She arched her hips towards it and moaned. "I *want*…"

"Then we'll do this the old-fashioned way." He leaned across her to open the drawer of the bedside cabinet. The weight of his chest crushing her breasts was intoxicating. "You underneath me like a good little wife."

"Yes," she hissed and bit lightly into his shoulder. "Quickly."

"Just a second," he murmured, snatching out a condom. "I need to take care of you."

"No need. I'm still protected by the pill I took this morning before the doctor told me to stop, so it's okay." She took the condom from his fingers and threw it on the carpet before spreading her legs wide and sliding the tip of her tongue between his lips. "And I don't feel sick any more. Come on, just this once, our wedding night…"

She felt her heart pounding wildly as he hesitated and pulled away until he was kneeling between her thighs. His eyes flickered over her naked body as she began to touch herself. His chest rose and fell as he watched. "You're sure?"

"It's *safe*," Helen persisted, licking her lips and rubbing the side of her foot up his thigh. "Now come on… "

"Okay, you win." Ricardo pushed her legs even wider with his hands. "Let me taste you first."

His mouth was hot and hard as she felt the stubble on his jaw rasp against the soft skin of her inner thighs. She closed her eyes and heard herself pant as his tongue parted her delicate folds, tasted, plunged, twisted and then withdrew to tease the inflamed nerve endings of her clitoris. She fisted her fingers into the black silk of his hair. "Stop, or I'll come," she said and pulled his head up. His shoulders followed and he put his hands on either side of her head as he kissed her, his tongue and lips still spiced with the flavor of her.

"Come on me instead," he muttered and she felt the wide tip of him nudge against her entrance. He eased himself in an inch and she felt his body tremble. "I don't want to hurt you."

"You won't." Her voice dropped an octave and she grasped his buttocks, her nails digging into the firm muscles. "Feel how wet you've made me, how much I want you."

He swore softly in Spanish and slid into her with one long thrust that made them both cry out with shock and pleasure. They were still for a moment, hearts pounding against each other. "*Dios*, are you sure about this?"

Her tone was desperate as she wrapped her legs around his hips and pushed her pubic bone into him hard. She clenched the muscles of her vagina around his penis until she felt him flex deep inside her. There was no way she could let him stop now. "Yes, damn you."

Ricardo entwined the fingers of both hands with hers and pushed them into the soft silk of the pillows as he began to slowly move inside her. His eyes bored down on her as her hips rose and fell to meet his. "You are a witch…"

"I'm anything you want me to be." She threw back her head and gasped as he thrust deeply into her, his length and girth taking her to a threshold of pain and pleasure she had never experienced before. "You make me want to—"

He untangled their fingers and slid his hands underneath her bottom to penetrate even deeper. His movements became faster as he gently pulled the cheeks apart and she wriggled with pleasure. "I make you want to what?"

"You make me want to…" Her body tensed like an iron spring as the force of his lovemaking pushed her deep into the mattress, his penis stretched and pulled her inside and out, igniting a million electrical nerve endings until there were no rules any more. "…scream." She felt herself splinter beneath him, gasping out his name, clawing at his skin as a lightning fast sensation hurled her into a rapid dark spiral of orgasm. Wave upon wave of convulsions shook her as he began to tumble after her, held tight in the darkness of her body, sliding, pulling and gripping her with intense force until she felt the violent heat of his release spread deep within her.

She clung to him in the afterglow, mind and body buzzing with adrenaline, hormones and emotions she couldn't even begin to fathom. The weight of his body made it difficult to breathe, but she didn't want the erotic imprisonment to end. "Dear God," she murmured against the soft skin of his chest.

"It will be slower next time," he said with a laugh and went to roll off her. "You forced me to come that quickly."

"No stay a moment." She squeezed him with her inner muscles. "I still want to feel you inside me."

He propped himself up on his shoulders to look at her. "You enjoyed it in the end then?"

Helen grinned. "It was worth the wait. I think I'm addicted."

"What made you change your mind? You didn't want complications a few hours ago."

She felt him stiffening once more inside her. "My wedding gift to you, Ricardo," she whispered and closed her eyes to the sensation of him pushing against her womb again. "Christ, you're good…"

"I can be better, slower." He nipped at her throat as she gasped with each firm stroke between her legs. "We're going to do this a lot, Mrs. Almanza. I'm going to make you come all over again." She cried out as he lifted her hips up from the mattress with his wide hands, impaling her deeply. "Lots of times." His pace quickened until all she could do was pant with wide-eyed pleasure. "Until you beg me to stop."

•

The sound of raised voices and rapid chatter outside on deck eventually woke Helen from a deep sleep.

Ricardo's voice was low and gruff as he pulled her closer against his chest under his arm. "That's the crew bringing us into dock. Don't worry. They won't disturb us until we're ready."

She yawned. "They must think we're spoiled, lazy wastrels just lying here while they flog. We should get up."

He slapped her bottom under the sheets. "It's our honeymoon for pity's sake. What do you think they'll be expecting us to do? Play Scrabble?"

She slapped him back. "I hadn't thought about that, smart ass."

And hadn't realized that we were behaving like a real *pair of besotted newlyweds.*

There was a loud clatter outside the door.

"*Dio!* The bloody cleaners already!" Ricardo heaved a resigned sigh with his massive shoulders. "I'm sorry, but I'm going to find it hard to concentrate properly on your exquisite little body with that racket going on."

Helen giggled at his irritation and pulled the sheet over her chest. "I think it's time to give in and show our faces, don't you?"

"I suppose so." He grunted, snatching up a conveniently placed robe. "But I'm not happy."

"But your staff will be when they actually see you. Everyone seems to adore you, Almanza, it's not just me…"

Ricardo looked at her quizzically for a moment and let out a small laugh. "Enough joking about, Helen. It's time you made me breakfast. I've had enough of fancy restaurants and takeaway junk food."

"Bloody chauvinist! In that case, there's something you really need to know."

"Go on."

"I'm a failure as a society wife." Helen clasped her hands together and grinned. "I can't cook, not in a socially acceptable way anyway. Sorry."

"I know." He chuckled as he decided against the robe, threw it on the floor, and reached for his discarded trousers.

"You do?"

"I've seen the state of your pantry in that hole in Ibiza, remember?"

"You've also been to dinner at my mum's. We have a lot in common, her and me."

Ricardo grinned and leaned over the bed to give her a kiss. "Your mum is lovely, and besides, there's more to life than food."

"Can any self respecting man say that?" Helen joked.

"He can when there's always a professional chef around, but hey, I did say your talents lay elsewhere. I don't want you getting all hot and bothered in the kitchen when you could be doing that in bed with me. And I can make coffee at least. We'll survive."

"You must buy pastries in that case."

"Guts." He threw her silk gown at her. "I'll shower later at the villa. Will you join me?"

"Am I safe?"

"No."

"Okay, it's a date."

"Come on then, let's get on shore."

They passed a couple of young women carrying baskets of fresh linen along the promenade deck. Large brown almond-shaped eyes, respectful yet adoring, gazed at their boss as he greeted them both by name. Helen heard their excited whispers as they scuttled away—they'd laid eyes on the new Senora Almanza!

The morning sun was dazzling, and the arc of gold and deep, deep blue that refused to be ignored took Helen's breath away. The bay was exquisite, rippling like molten glass, blue, green, and gold beneath the fading dawn sky. "Oh my God," she whispered.

"Approve?"

"And the rest! It's like something out of a top end holiday brochure, airbrushed with a top coat of glitter."

"*Bueno*."

"Gorgeous…"

"There are no designer shops, I'm afraid."

"Good."

"No British booze, either."

Helen paused for thought and then shot him a playful look. "I'll live."

"Very patchy Internet and mobile phone reception."

"Oh do stop it and hurry up!" She slapped him on the shoulder with her sun hat. "You promised me a shower."

Chapter Eight

A speedboat took them to an old wooden quay. The bay was far too shallow for a yacht the size of *Indalo* to get near to shore. Helen arrived breathless and more tangle-headed than she'd previously been, and the short bumpy sprint to shore left her exhilarated. She shouldn't have been as overawed by this level of luxury but she was. High cliffs smothered in trees surrounded the bay, but as she craned her neck towards the clouds she could see a rooftop peeking through the foliage, a few tantalizing tiles and a round white curve of stone.

"There's a house," she said and pointed as he took her hand to help her out of the boat.

"That's the observatory."

"Observatory?"

"Yes, built by an astronomer forced to retire to sunnier climates by a very bossy wife."

"Fascinating!"

Ricardo chuckled and gestured towards an open-topped Jeep attended by a slight man wearing dark glasses and Bermuda shorts. "Come on, we can walk it, but it'll be a lot quicker if I drive."

"You're the boss."

Ricardo took the keys from the man who nodded and left without saying a word. "You mean that?"

"Of course not." She laughed. "But let's get a move on, shall we?"

"Welcome to Dizzy Heights," Ricardo said after driving at top speed up a steep winding road through dense pine trees that were now clearing to reveal a high-gated entrance.

Helen blinked. She saw the bright blue of a sky that could only have its feet in the sea. The light was infused with ozone and Mediterranean sparkle. She breathed in deeply as her brain registered all the color — sand and honey-colored stones on one side, smooth whitewashed walls on the other, purple bougainvillea, deep green myrtle and scarlet hibiscus.

"This is the upper entrance," Ricardo said as he brought the Jeep to a halt. "The lower one is for deliveries and staff use."

"A staff entrance?" she asked incredulously.

"I suppose that's what it is." He switched off the engine.

"Dear God, this place is huge. Another of your investment new-builds?"

"Oh no, not this one. This is home, in a special green zone. It's safe from new development forever."

"A touch ironic considering all your other properties."

"Yes, you could say hypocritical too if you like, and I'll understand."

"Would you?"

"You don't think I'm not lashed by criticism on a daily basis do you? I am. People hate me for what I do."

"For what you do?"

"Think about it. I'm a banker and a builder. I buy up land with my financial profits, build houses, and then lend people the money to buy them off me. It upsets people, even rich ones, especially the ones with lots and lots of land right next door."

"And it doesn't bother you?"

Ricardo shrugged. "I don't let it. It's business and I have no desire to be poor." He held out a hand to help Helen out of the car. "But enough of this serious talk, we're supposed to be enjoying ourselves."

The smell of wood smoke drifted towards them, and Helen noticed a blue wisp coming from a chimney towards one end of the house. "Looks like we have company already," she said brightly, trying to hide her disappointment.

"Lucia, my housekeeper will be making us bread and preparing a selection of meals for us should we require them later." He ignored her gasp of surprise as he grabbed her by the waist and pulled her tightly into him as they walked. "She'll be gone in under an hour, don't worry."

"I wasn't worried."

"And none of the staff will return to the main house until I tell them to. I value my privacy, that's why I bought such a huge estate. Plenty of room for everyone. Peace and quiet."

"It sounds wonderful."

"We'll find Lucia in the kitchen." Ricardo guided her down a flight of steep steps down the side of the villa towards an open doorway. "Right through here."

A portly, middle-aged woman with salt and pepper hair neatly arranged in a bun was working furiously at a huge ball of dough on a long wooden table. She looked up with a start as Ricardo surprised her from behind with a bear hug that crushed her wrinkled cheeks into his shoulder.

"Great to see you, Lucia." He outstretched an arm to beckon Helen closer. "And this, my dear old friend, is my new wife, Helen."

The older woman looked her up and down and nodded.

"So it's true, the rumors. You finally got married. Not to one of those orange-skinned stick insects, thank God."

"Isn't she beautiful?"

"Helen, you say?" Lucia turned to look Ricardo in the eye with a frown on her lips. "Quite a name. It means a shining light as I recall."

Helen felt her cheeks flush. She flashed a smile she hoped the other woman would mirror. Lucia did not oblige and Ricardo continued to grin regardless of the insult. "Pleased to meet you, Lucia."

"She certainly is!" Ricardo said interrupting. "Cooking isn't one of her talents apparently."

Lucia harrumphed and wriggled free from under Ricardo's shoulder and started to pound the large ball of dough again. She punched it hard, sending a puff of flour into the air. "We can only hope she is good at other things then can't we, *muchacho*?"

Ricardo laughed. "You know me too well."

Lucia shot him a sideways glance that had the beginnings of a wry smile, but completely ignored Helen. "Get out of my kitchen and go play like a good boy," she grumbled. "Let me know when you want dinner."

"I'm really not at all hungry." Helen crossed her arms across her chest. For the first time in her life she wished she was a bloody cordon bleu cook just to put this woman's superior old nose out of joint. She glared at Ricardo hard until her eyeballs hurt.

"Ah, yes," Ricardo said, his eyes flitting from one woman to the other appearing to sense that this situation needed delicate handling. "Helen, *tesoro*, why don't you take yourself up to the pool and I'll bring you something to drink in a few minutes?"

Helen took the hint immediately and was relieved to be

leaving the domain that was clearly not intended to be hers. The pool was easy to find around the back of the house, an enormous infinity one with spectacular views over the bay below.

Feeling in a very bad mood and also feeling annoyingly hungry, Helen lowered herself down to the pool edge, kicked off her sandals, and dipped her feet into the deep clear water. As smooth ripples lapped around her ankles, a flash reflected up from the water. It was the morning sun hitting the massive diamond on her hand. It no longer seemed ostentatious, not here. Everything about Ricardo's life was big and expensive. The biggest and the best, even down to his lovemaking, the hum of her aching muscles was testament to that. Correction: not lovemaking, but wildly intense, consensual sex. The word love wasn't part of their deal.

She held the ring a little closer. It was astonishingly beautiful, large clear flawless facets. She'd never looked at it closely in daylight before. Talk about marrying in haste! The stone itself was the size of a small mosaic tile, square with its rounded edges set in gold. She twisted it around and noticed an interruption in the smooth yellow metal mount. Squinting in the sunlight she made out some engraving. A lion's head, similar to the cufflinks Ricardo had been wearing when their worlds had first collided in the Condesa's boudoir. Helen laughed at the memory. She had sincerely thought he was about to kill her, but then she went and married her so-called assailant!

The lion's head had to be an Almanza crest of some sort. It suited him. He too was ferocious, proud, and magnificent. She twisted the ring in the opposite direction expecting to see a matching cat, but there was a different shape entirely. It was a flower. Looking at the leaves and the shape of its petals, it was just like a primrose... Helen swallowed. Did they have primroses in Spain? Or was it a reference to Primrose Farm? It had to be. Ricardo must have had the ring specially made for her. But surely even the keenest paparazzi lens couldn't pick out such an intimate detail? Why had he done such a thing?

She was surprisingly moved by the gesture. The man had made quite an effort in the few days before their hasty wedding. He had also pointed out the clause in the pre-nup that insisted all clothes, accessories, and jewelry were hers to keep. And she would. The ring was probably worth a fortune in scrap alone, but she'd never sell it. Ricardo had given it to her, and it was special.

Her pleasure faded quickly, however, as she remembered the precise details of when he'd given her the ring. He hadn't gone down on one knee, said he loved her and pleaded for her hand. No, not quite. He'd chucked it at her and left the room without a backwards glance to see if she even liked it. Helen sighed sadly and closed her eyes against the bright sunshine.

This was a business deal with the added bonus of some hot sex thrown in. Three months was enough to keep up appearances. Could a honeymoon last that long? There were so many unasked questions about this marriage.

"Food!"

Helen's nose twitched as Ricardo slid a plate of warm sugar-coated pastries and a cup of coffee down beside her on a wooden tray. "I'm not sure I dare try one of those," she murmured.

"And why not?"

"Because Lucia hates me. She'll have slung some Menorcan hemlock in there."

Ricardo bit lavishly down into one of the sweet morsels and Helen's mouth began to water as crispy flakes crumbled down the front of his T-shirt. "Death by cake sounds fine to me," he said.

Helen snatched up a round one with a glossy half moon of yellow nestling in its center. "Greedy bloody sod."

"Hmmm."

"I hope you choke," she muttered with half a smile and closed her eyes as buttery almonds, vanilla, and peach melted like sin on her tongue.

"If I go before you do, darling," he said with a grin, "you'll be a very rich woman. A merry widow who won't have to worry about cooking for herself ever again."

"Rubbish. If your lawyer hasn't covered your sudden death by cake then he should be struck off." She accepted the fat china cup of café con leche that he handed her. "Anyway, I didn't know you were a banker."

"You don't know that much about me at all." He helped himself to a cigar-shaped delight with a chocolate center. "This is a marriage of convenience, remember?"

Helen laughed in spite of herself. "Fair enough, I deserved that."

"Lucia doesn't hate you, for what it's worth."

"I'd never have guessed."

"You should have a chat with her newest daughter-in-law. Believe me, you have no idea how protective Menorcan mamas can be. Anyway, you can relax, she just went home."

"Does she ever smile?"

"After and during cider she does."

Helen snorted. "Blimey, I'd like to see that!"

"Stick around until the next family celebration and you just might, along with her husband's famous spit roast pork. It's the only time she doesn't cook, because she's too…happy." His eyebrows lifted at the sound of a telephone ringing inside the house. "Who the hell is that? I don't think that phone's rung in about three years!"

Helen watched as he marched quickly through an arch on the terrace and waited silently until the sound of ringing stopped. She wondered if she would be around when the next family celebration occurred. Part of her hoped there would be one within the next three months.

Ricardo's harsh voice behind her made her jump. "I need you to swallow that mouthful and be very brave." His expression was serious. "I'm sorry to have to ask, but I think I might need your help."

"What's happened?"

"Lucia's son, her eldest, his house is on fire. His wife and kids are inside and he's trying to get to them, but the staircase has collapsed. The emergency services are on their way, but we're nearer—"

Helen leaped to her feet and snatched up her bag. "Come on, let's go."

• • •

Perhaps he should have left her behind.

He had no idea what would be waiting for them when they arrived at Tino's farm. It could be unpleasant. Distressing. Traumatic. But it was too late now. They were in the middle of nowhere and about five minutes away from a burning building with no civilization in between.

He had to break the silence. "Are you okay?"

Helen turned to face him, her hair whipping across her face as the Jeep lurched forward over the rough road surface. "I'm the last person you should be worrying about!" she shouted over the noise of flying grit and a hot engine.

"That's good to hear." He hoped she was right as his heart skipped a beat at what lay ahead. She stared in front of her and he could see a muscle working in her jaw. "There's the smoke. We'll be there in a couple of minutes."

The Jeep skidded to a halt in a shower of grit a few yards from the burning farmhouse. "No flames this side!" Ricardo shouted as he leaped out of the driver's seat and began to run towards the building. "Must be round the back. Tino!"

He didn't hear Helen reply as his feet pounded the rock hard mud drive, but this was no time for social niceties. He wasn't panicking, but his heart was full of dread at the prospect of what was around the corner. Why did things like this always seem to happen to the nice people?

Ricardo saw Tino standing with his arms raised to the sky on the back terrace.

"Senor Almanza! *Gracias a Dios*! Thank God!"

Blood trickled down the man's face, a scarlet trail through grey ash and red soil. His breath came in short bursts. "I've tried to get up there by the ladder, but it slips on the terrace. The marble—"

"Where are they?"

Tino pointed to an open window two floors up. "Estrella is in the bathroom, with the children, safer there. She wouldn't throw the baby down, she couldn't do it. She said she was going to soak towels in water, but I keep shouting for her and she's stopped calling back." Tino's voice cracked. "I'm so scared, senor."

"How long since she spoke?"

"A few minutes. Just before I heard your car."

"Quickly, the ladder!" Ricardo shouted as he dragged it up off the ground and propped it up against the wall underneath the bathroom window. "Wedge your feet against the bottom and hold it steady so it doesn't slip again. I'll go up."

"No, senor, it is too dangerous. Let me."

Ricardo had been the first to find dead bodies once before. He wasn't going to let another human being go through that.

"I'm taller and stronger than you, Tino. And you're bleeding everywhere. You'll frighten them all. Just hold the ladder." He shot him a stern look and ignored the nausea he was feeling. "Now!"

The wooden ladder wobbled as he climbed it as quickly and safely as possible, blocking out the sensation of heat he could feel emanating from the building. He thanked God that the old building didn't have modern tiny inaccessible bathroom windows. He'd be able to climb inside reasonably easily.

"Estrella!"

Nothing. His hands shook as he gripped the rough window frame and hauled himself head first inside. There was gray brown smoke. He coughed, the air scraped at his throat and tongue. In the corner of the bathroom was a huddle of fabric. Wet twisted towels and four sleeping angels.

Twenty seconds of agony elapsed before Ricardo could establish they were all still alive but unconscious. The pressure inside his skull was so intense he could hardly think straight. Exhaling with relief, he made the sign of the cross across his heart before prying the baby from her mother's arms and then ran choking to the window. The bundle in his hands was hot, damp, and felt too heavy for something so small. The smoke grew thicker and more acrid as Helen and Tino stared anxiously up at him.

"Helen, hold the ladder. Tino, up here quickly!"

Tino was visibly shaking as he scrambled up the ladder, tears spilling over his lower lashes. "Is she—"

"They're all alive, but we must be quick." He carefully handed over the baby and smiled encouragingly as she started to cry. "Take her to Helen and come back up and help me."

"First aid kit!" Helen yelled up at him. "Got one in the car?"

"Under the dashboard," he said, his voice sounding harsher than he intended. "But not until they're all out and down!"

Two more trips and Ricardo was carrying down Estrella over his shoulder as the sound of sirens and engines came at last. Ricardo stood back and silently watched as the professionals took over, catching his breath and willing his heart rate to slow down now the situation was under control.

He felt a cool hand on his forearm. "You saved their lives," Helen whispered.

"They would have been okay." Ricardo closed his eyes for a few seconds. "We should go now."

Chapter Nine

Ricardo was silent and stony-faced on the journey back to the villa, and Helen couldn't think of anything to say under the circumstances. General chitchat felt inappropriate. The man she had seen in action wasn't the shallow playboy billionaire she'd thought she'd married. He'd shown extraordinary strength and self-control under pressure, and his hands weren't shaking with the shock of it all like hers were.

They'd stayed an hour or so after the ambulance left, and Ricardo had made sure there was somebody to deal with every aspect of the farm while Tino was at the hospital. The animals still had to be fed and stabled, clothes and toiletries would need to be taken to the hospital, phone calls needed to be made, forms filled out…the list seemed endless.

"I need a drink. I don't know about you," he said as they arrived back at the villa. He suddenly looked completely drained. "A large one."

"Just what the doctor ordered," Helen said and tried to keep up as he strode across the drive towards the front door.

Once inside the living room, its glass doors flung open to the warm sea breeze and cry of seabirds. Ricardo handed her a large tumbler of whiskey before knocking his own back in one go. His voice was gravely. "Sorry, did you want ice?"

"It's okay, I'll get some." She sniffed the smoky liquid. "I'll need a dash of lemonade from the kitchen if I'm going to swallow this lot and live."

"Sorry, there's other stuff," he said and ran his forearm across the soot and sweat on his the forehead. "Come on, let's see what we can find in there. The fridge is always full."

Helen noticed a tremor in his hand as she gave him back her glass. "You have that and then go and have a long hot bath. I can manage a fridge door on my own."

"Thanks." He sipped the second whiskey more slowly. "Sure you don't mind?"

"Of course not, as long as Lucia's not guarding it!"

"Lucia has her hands full with her family right now. I've given her as much time off as she needs. But she'll be your best friend forever after what you did today, don't worry." He drained his glass and put it down with a click on a glass table.

"I didn't do much."

He shook his head. "You were there for me," he said quietly. "And for Tino and his family. There to help, no questions asked. Not many women I've known would have done that, risked ruining their expensive manicures and hairstyles."

Helen glanced down at her hands. Her wedding manicure was a distant memory. She had a torn nail and the rest were full of dirt. "I think I'd better wash these while I'm in the kitchen," she said laughing. "And then have a bath myself."

"Good idea," Ricardo said and turned to leave. "I'll see you later."

Later? That didn't sound like an invitation to join him with a bar of soap. Helen shrugged and tried to put her disappointment aside. Thinking he might want her to join him for anything other than sex was irrational, not to mention stupid. She had no right to try to comfort him after the trauma of the fire, or indeed seek comfort herself. This was a business relationship, not an emotional one. She'd feel better after that drink.

•

"Do you like seafood?" Ricardo asked as he finished preparing the wood oven on the terrace. "The charcoal will be white-hot and ready in about half an hour."

Helen was staring out to sea, the newspaper she had been reading folded neatly on the table beside her. She turned her head to look at him as he approached. "Depends what it is," she said cautiously, her bright green eyes sparkling like glass in the afternoon sun.

Ricardo drew up a chair beside her and placed a glass jug and two highball glasses on the table. "Perhaps it would be easier to tell me what you do and don't like then."

"No whelks or oysters, not that I've ever been brave enough or drunk enough to try them."

"But they're supposed to make you horny," he said and felt a zing of pleasure when she rewarded him with a broad grin.

Helen snorted. "Whelks? Yeah, right, like gagging is romantic."

"I meant the oysters. I've never had whelks either, I don't think."

"They look like massive snails with disgusting looking gray and yellow innards." She made a retching noise. "My granny used to pry them out with a pin and drown them in vinegar."

Her face was a picture of revulsion and he couldn't

help letting a small laugh escape. "Actually, they do sound disgusting."

"They have to be looking like that, don't they?"

"I was going to suggest grilling some local red prawns scattered with garlic oil and flakes of sea salt, but if you'd prefer steak ribs—"

"Oh no, they sound perfect!"

Ricardo took her small hand in his and rubbed his thumb across the surface of the diamond on her ring finger. "You washed your hands."

"I washed *everything*," she said provocatively. "I found a bathroom on my way to the kitchen and it looked so inviting…"

He lifted her hand, twisted it and kissed the inside of her wrist. The skin was delicate and soft, her pulse like the touch of a butterfly's wing against his lips. "You look and smell wonderful."

"Thank you," she murmured. Color tinted her cheeks, spreading like pink ink dropped in water. "You have immaculate taste in toiletries."

"I have immaculate taste in everything," he said silkily. "Especially where women are concerned."

Helen frowned playfully and pulled her hand away. "I bet you say that to all the girls, you feckless swine."

Ricardo chuckled. "I love it when you insult me like that, wife."

Her eyes widened with mock outrage, and she smacked his forearm with the newspaper. "Make that 'you feckless *pervert* swine'!"

Ricardo just laughed and began to pour from the jug. "How come nobody's married you before now, Helen? I'm baffled." Ice cubes clanked and bubbles leapt over the rim of the Murano glassware.

"I'm only twenty-four, Ricardo. Give a girl a chance!"

"Seriously, though. I saw the way Hippy looked at you, you can't have ever been short of boyfriends looking like you do."

"Stop fishing about, Almanza, and ask me what you really want to know." Her emerald gaze held him fast, and he was lost for words for a second or two. She was as sharp as needles.

"Okay, how many men in your life?" There, he'd said it, she'd made him. He wanted to know.

"It's really none of your business."

"So?" He did his most persuasive smile, dropped his hand to her knee and began to stroke it.

She sighed. "Four. None of them particularly serious or long lasting. I moved around a lot with university and travel, and looking back, I think all of them were only after one thing."

"You mean—"

She gestured at her chest, molded into stunning curves by the bronze beaded bodice of her sundress. "I've been led to believe I have great tits, but I'm not exactly good marriage material."

"Seriously?"

"For real." She picked up her glass and sniffed. "And to save you asking, my first time was at a young farmers' party after too much cider. In a barn. Now, what is this potion you've given me?"

"Pomada, Mahon gin, lemonade, sugar syrup and a slice of lemon." A shutter had come down behind her eyes. She was putting him at arm's length and it served him right. It *was* none of his business. Not unless he proved himself better than the previous four. "And the hippy? Was he number four?"

"No, he was not!"

"Are you sure?"

Her tone was a touch irritable. "Of course I'm sure, Ricardo. I'm not a mentalist. I do know what I'm doing most of the time."

"You met him on an archaeological course, you said. That is an unusual recreation for a young woman in Ibiza, you have to admit."

"You think so?" She took a long drink from her glass and took a moment before swallowing. "Ooh, that *is* nice."

She was trying to politely change the subject, but he had developed a strong dislike of her dodgy friend Bjorn. It wasn't jealousy. It was merely concern driving him to uncover everything about their relationship, that's all. "Tell me about it."

"Archaeology's always interested me, ever since my grandparents bought me a metal detector for Christmas when I was nine. I'd spend hours wandering around the fields and estuary looking for stuff. Once you're bitten by the bug it's hard to stop."

"Did you find anything valuable?"

Helen laughed. "If I'd found a big hoard of treasure, I wouldn't have had to marry you, would I?"

"I guess not."

"I did find some old clay smoking pipes though and some broken pottery, and lots of rubbish."

"And with the hippy? Did you find any fascinating artifacts together?"

"His name is Bjorn, and yes we found some very nice things. Some of the groups' Phoenician-Punic finds are being displayed in the Archaeological Museum in the Old Town. Do you know it?"

"The one by the cathedral, yes, I know it well, but haven't been inside for a long time."

"We should go. I could show you the bits we unearthed."

He tried to suppress a frown but failed miserably. He really didn't have time for this Bjorn character and he didn't want Helen to either. "You and him?"

"The entire group. There are about twenty of us." Helen sighed. "If I didn't know better, I'd say you were jealous."

"That would be a preposterous conclusion. I don't trust him, that's all."

"You've barely met him, how can you possibly judge?"

"I saw the way he looked at you. The way he spoke. The way he touched you."

Anger bubbled up inside him and the words came out before he could stop them. "And he said something about 'only two weeks ago' you were doing something that made him surprised you were suddenly married. What conclusion am I supposed to come to with that?"

"That we've been at it like rabbits on acid obviously!"

"Well?"

Helen braced her hands on the arms of the chair as if to stand up. "Well *what*?"

"What did he mean by that?"

"I haven't a clue, Ricardo, perhaps he was just trying to wind you up? Perhaps he didn't like the look of my new married-in-haste husband. Maybe he suspected you were after one thing, or my money!" She laughed humorlessly. "This conversation is starting to get on my nerves."

She was right. He was behaving like a control freak. What the hell was wrong with him? "I'm sorry," he murmured. "It's been a shit day."

Helen was silent for a moment and then her expression softened. "Then let's not make it any worse." To his surprise she reached across and put her hand over his. It was soft and cool. It felt good. "I have an idea."

"Tell me more," he said, feeling calmer.

"Lucia isn't going to be here for a while, right?" She feigned a gasp of horror and slapped the back of her hand against her forehead dramatically. "Which means we have to fend for ourselves?"

He couldn't stop a smile escaping. "Don't worry, you're in good hands."

She grinned broadly. "I thought you'd say something like that, so how about you teach me to cook?"

"There's no need, Helen. I like to cook now and again, and when I don't we can get someone else to do it, or go out, or order in. You don't need to cook any more."

"Not for three months I don't," she said with a wry smile. "But consider this. If you teach me to cook I might snag myself a *real* husband one day. A husband that loves me."

That remark shouldn't have hurt quite as much as it did. It was a sharp, sudden pain that caught him unawares. It unsettled him, and he wasn't sure why. That was the deal, after all. Three months and they were done. "Then there's no time like the present. Let's go fetch those prawns."

"Deal," she said and stood up. He looked up into her smiling face. He'd not seen her from that angle before. She was beautiful. The underside of her chin was a perfect triangle, and like alabaster. He wanted to taste it. "And Ricardo," she whispered playfully. "Bjorn is gay."

• • •

Helen ran her fingers along the grain of the kitchen table and watched with fascination as Ricardo rummaged through the fridge. "Tell me about your friend, Jerardo."

"Jerardo?" He shot her a puzzled look over his shoulder and then resumed his search.

"Yes, our best man."

Ricardo let out a sharp laugh. "That's not why he was there, Helen. He needed to be present to make sure I really did get married! He's not a friend."

Helen caught the bulb of garlic he tossed in her direction. "I did think he was probably a bit old to be a mate, but I didn't know what else to call him."

Ricardo laughed. "Conniving old bastard will do."

"What did you do to him to make him hate you so much?" She looked at the garlic bulb curiously and sniffed it.

"I never did anything to him. Now wash this parsley under the tap, will you?"

She took the bunch of cool green herbs from him and wandered over to the sink. "So why did he blackmail you into getting married against your will? What was in it for him?"

"Revenge. Cold, hard-hearted revenge. Whatever it cost him. Even though my father's dead now, he clearly feels the need to try and punish the entire Almanza line."

"So your dad did something to him?" She turned the tap on too quickly and water splashed up over her arms and chest. "Damn!"

He laughed at the state of her. "Persistent creature, aren't you?"

"And wet!" Helen grinned. "Just tell me what happened!"

Ricardo sighed and leaned against the edge of the sink next to her. "Jerardo and my father were business partners many years ago. Jerardo put up the capital in the early days, spoiled rich kid that he was, and my father was the business brains and the charisma. To cut a long story short, my dad stole Jerardo's fiancée and married her himself, and he never forgave him."

Helen's tone softened as he dabbed at her wet collarbone with a dry cloth. "So your mother was supposed to marry

Jerardo?"

"No, my mother was divorced by my father so he could marry the Condesa. The Condesa, your old boss, was the 'other woman' and Jerardo's fiancée. They both wanted her for her title and aristocratic connections even though her ennobled family was penniless. She was also well known for being a complete whore in bed. They found her irresistible."

"How awkward…"

"More than that, I'm afraid. There were rumors that the Condesa was carrying Jerardo's unborn child, but aborted it, a double whammy. The whole affair tore their social networks apart, and my dad ended up in prison. Jerardo had allies in dark places, friends with power that could be bought. They framed my father and ensured he was convicted of fraud and embezzlement. He was banged up for twenty years, but only survived in that hell hole of a prison for three."

He looked terribly sad all of a sudden and Helen struggled for the right words, but found none that would suffice. "What a dreadful mess."

Ricardo shrugged and looked out of the kitchen window towards the sea. "All he asked of me before he died was to get the department store back and do my best to clear the family name. I'm half way there now, thanks to you."

"Honor."

He paused for a moment and watched her shake the water from the parsley. "Yes."

"I think I understand it all a bit more now." She felt awkward, but the question had to be asked. "Weren't you angry about what your dad did to your mum?"

Ricardo frowned. "He was still my father, whatever he'd done. He gave me life."

"So did your mother."

Ricardo nodded and sent her a knowing look. "She did,

but she was no angel either."

"Perhaps I'd better not ask any more questions right now. I'm getting hungry."

His body visibly relaxed. "You're always hungry."

"There's always something good to eat when you're around, that's why."

"Well, tonight you're going to help. We'll get you cooking up a storm in no time." He produced a mortar and pestle. "Peel the garlic, chuck in some of these salt crystals, and bash it all up until I tell you to stop."

A few minutes later Helen plunged down the stubby wooden pestle and a clove of garlic flew into to air. "Told you I was hopeless…"

"Just a little too enthusiastic," he said and moved to stand behind her. She felt his breath on her neck as he reached around and took her hands in his, guiding her until they had established a steady grinding rhythm. "There, you see. You just need to be a little more gentle, take your time…"

Helen closed her eyes and savored the feel of his body, warm and hard against her back. "It smells amazing."

"And then we throw in some of this parsley that I've chopped for you…"

"And keep grinding?"

His voice had become low and husky. "Just stir now while I dribble in some of this virgin olive oil." She could feel a distinct ridge pushing into the small of her back and a spark of lust made her blood flare. "Nice circular movements, that's it, use your hips if it helps. And when it feels loose and slippery it's ready."

"You bastard." Helen dropped the pestle and spun round to pull his mouth down on hers. Their tongues meshed angrily as she crushed her breasts against his chest willing him to push harder against her. Squeezed between the edge of the heavy kitchen table and the hardness of his erection was exactly where she wanted to be, where she wanted him to have her again. "You know exactly what you're doing."

"I don't know what you mean," he said but she could feel his lips form into a smile as he lifted the skirt of her bohemian sundress.

Her breath was already coming in gasps as she fumbled with the zip of his black chinos. "You turned me on deliberately. Underhanded, not at all gentlemanly."

"Then we have gone far enough," he said and pulled away from her embrace and carefully lowered her dress back down.

"What?"

"I don't keep condoms in the kitchen, my darling, and I'm supposed to be teaching you how to cook."

"But—"

"And I'm not just after one thing like all the others." He kissed the top of her shoulder lightly. "I want to prove that to you."

"Don't you want to, here on the kitchen table? It would be so incredibly erotic."

"Later," he said and gave her a look of mock admonishment. "Build the excitement, layer by layer. It's more fun that way. For both of us."

"You're cruel," she whispered, but rewarded him with a provocative smile.

"But I'm always right."

·

"My mum would love this," Helen said an hour later as she dropped the last prawn shell onto her plate.

"Well, now you know how, you can cook it for her often," Ricardo said. "Quite simple really, wasn't it?"

"Yep, except I'm not sure we can source prawns quite like that at home or the sunset."

"It is beautiful, that's why I'm always drawn back here. Among other things."

"Such as?"

"Friends, nostalgia…it's the place I consider my real home."

Helen giggled. "You *do* seem to have a lot of houses."

"Bricks and mortar, some of them, that's all."

"And marble, alabaster, custom-made sheets of the finest Venetian glass…"

Ricardo held up a hand as a gesture of defeat. "Fair enough, but there's a certain feeling about home, isn't there? You must have it with Primrose Farm."

"I will confess to missing a decent cup of tea outside England, that's for sure!" She picked up her wine glass and stared out to sea, squinting as the fiery red sun melted into the deep blue of the sea. "But I can't pretend I don't enjoy sunnier climates. The air seems a lot purer, especially near the sea, and it's much drier than at home. Less humidity. I love the feel of the sun on my skin in the morning. Being cold and wet for over half the year is vastly overrated."

"But an excuse for snuggling up in front of a blazing log fire."

"Ah, so romantic. I grew up with log fires. The wood was free and coal far too expensive. In fact, doing the ashes every morning was one of my chores as a child. But it was a necessity, not a luxury. You won't have noticed because we didn't stay the night and you only got as far as the kitchen, but Primrose Farm has no central heating. It gets bloody cold."

"You get used to it, I imagine."

"I never knew any differently until I went to other people's houses that were too hot with stale air and thick carpets and electrical cables everywhere." She shuddered. "God knows what their fuel bills must have been like."

"So your folks are pretty much self sufficient?"

"They have to be, they own the place, but there's never been much spare cash." *They own the place now I've cleared their debts.* "It's not a life I'd choose to lead."

"Really? You'd rather work for someone like my wicked step-mother?"

Helen laughed. "I wouldn't go that far, but farming isn't as idyllic as people would have you believe. I love the farm, it's the only home I've ever known, but I want to do other things in my life too. It means I've had to be a bit selfish if I'm honest, which isn't a nice feeling."

"How so?"

"Once dad can't run the farm anymore there's no one to take over. I'm an only child, no big strapping brothers, no wholesome, ruddy-cheeked son-in-law to pick up the slack." She shrugged and looked away. "I can't make that sort of sacrifice, and mum's made it clear she doesn't want me to follow in her footsteps either. I don't want to be a farmer, and I certainly don't want to be a farmer's wife."

"But they seemed so happy together, your parents."

"Oh they are! They adore each other, absolutely devoted. You have to be leading a life like that. Do you know what Mum always says? 'The dawn chorus is the most beautiful sound on God's earth when you're up at four every day, but the only time your father and I have been away from this farm overnight was on our honeymoon. Thirty years ago. See the world, Helen. Do *everything*. Do it for me.'" Helen blinked and pressed her lips resolutely together as he studied her. "She says it to me every time I go home so that I don't forget."

"She's right, Helen. It's their choice to live that way. You must follow your heart and do what's right for you."

"The guilt is overwhelming sometimes. Stupid, isn't it?"

"You're very sweet. Not stupid."

Helen took a deep breath and stretched out her legs beneath the table. The night sky was beginning to twinkle with stars, splintered diamonds on blue velvet. The scent of night blossoms was becoming intense. "I'm now feeling decidedly *not* sweet."

Ricardo grinned and looked at her mischievously over the rim of his wine glass. "Should I be afraid?"

"You promised me a shower this morning, remember?"

"I did?"

Helen stood up and sent him a long look that she hoped spelled it out in big bold lettering. "Yes, you know very well you did, and now I really, really want it." Her heart began to pound as he followed her lead, rose from his seat, and was suddenly very close.

"There were eight bathrooms in the place the last time I counted," he said silkily and traced a warm fingertip across the top of her shoulder. One spaghetti strap slid off. "Where would you like to start?"

She felt as if her skin was on fire and hoped her eyes were smoldering sufficiently for him to guess that she didn't just want to get clean. "The nearest one will do very nicely."

"I see." he slipped the other strap off and the silk slipped silently to her waist. "No bra?"

Her heart rate kicked up as he stared down at her exposed breasts. "No bra."

She heard her own breath catch as he took both nipples between his fingers and began to tease them into hard sensitive peaks. "You're very dirty, Helen. I think you're right, an immediate shower is in order."

She reached between his legs to confirm an unmistakable erection. "You're filthy too, Almanza."

"I certainly feel that way," he whispered and lowered his mouth to the sensitive spot between her shoulder and neck. "Let's fix that, shall we?"

Helen allowed a small moan to escape as he bit lightly into her flesh, sending tiny electrical darts of pleasure to the apex of her thighs. "Yes…"

The next few moments were a blur, but somehow they found themselves naked and in the master bedroom with Ricardo holding open the door to an enormous wet room. He turned on the jets, pulled Helen inside, and shut the door firmly behind them. His mouth had covered hers before she could say a single word.

Helen closed her eyes beneath the sharp hot darts of water and felt herself weaken as his hard body brushed up against her, the coarse hair of his thighs, large eager hands exploring her contours, his tongue exploring her mouth and a huge penis nudging up between her legs. "Let me wash you," he murmured and trickled cold shower gel over her breasts.

She tensed for a moment, thrilling at the contrasting sensation of hot and cold, enraptured by the exotic scent of expensive essential oils. And then she felt the roughness of his hands spread the slippery potion over her nipples, teasing and plucking as he went. "Yes…"

"Hush," he murmured, silencing her with his mouth and began to spread the lather down over her rib cage, around her back, over her buttocks and then massaged the bubbles into the triangle of hair between her thighs. She tried to touch him back, but he took hold of her hands and folded them behind her neck. "Not me this time," he muttered. "Just you."

She slithered a little as he pushed her gently up against the tiled wall, water gushing in torrents over them both, sensitizing her entire body with sharp little pulses of sensation. She felt the small mosaic tiles pressing into the back of her hands behind her neck, then into the soft flesh of her shoulder blades until her buttocks were pressed up against the wall too by his powerful hips and hands. "Stay just like that," he said. "No touching me."

"But I want to." She opened her eyes to see the dark thunder in his eyes as he lowered his head to kiss her breasts, slowly, first one then the other, sucking each one hard until she shuddered and gasped.

"You may not touch me. Not this time."

He slid one large hand behind her bottom against the wall and his other slipped quickly between her legs. She heard herself whimper as he put two fingers against her entrance, stroked them languorously back and forth brushing her clitoris and coating every part of her sex with foam. "Ricardo," she muttered helplessly and then gasped as his fingers entered her. "I want to—"

"No," his voice was harsh as he inserted a third finger, and his thumb began to rub her clitoris in delirious circles. "Not until I've watched you come."

Helen lost the power of speech and the ability to resist him almost immediately. The feel of him pushing in, out and around inside her was unbearably erotic. His thumb was sending bolts of untamed energy to her breasts, crushing the breath out of her lungs with desire. Her thighs became weak and soft as his strong hands pushed her sex up against and into the wall with the motion of his thrusts and she opened them wider for him than she thought possible. No pain, no discomfort just blinding lust. "I want you inside me, Ricardo, please."

"Not yet," he said and began to use his entire body to urge her onwards. "Relax, let me do this for you, let go, come on me hard."

She felt his chest rasp against her nipples, pressing

urgently against her full wet breasts, his erection hot and hard against the base of her stomach, pushing into her hip, his balls so close to her center she could feel their soft weight against her skin. She was ready. "Yes, more."

His voice was guttural. "That's it, shout if you want to, it turns me on."

Helen groaned loudly as he took a nipple deep into his mouth. "Harder," she said and felt her hips buck involuntarily. "Yes, really hard." Pleasure devoured her as her body was consumed by his touch. His hands, his mouth, even his breath against her skin was igniting her. And then the world turned black for a few seconds as she felt herself shatter into a spiraling orgasm. His voice became muffled as she cried out his name and an intense sensation spread throughout her body, rippling like waves of sin. Pure, decadent, selfish adult pleasure.

He held her close against him as her climax subsided, letting the water slide down and between them, washing away the foam until her skin felt squeaky. His tongue tasted sweet as he continued to kiss her and then the water stopped. "You're clean now. Let me dry you."

Helen silently allowed him to wrap her in a black cotton towel and carry her to the bed. He laid her down and she watched as he slowly dried himself in front of her, paying particular attention to the area below his taut, bronzed stomach. He was just inches from her face. "You're massive," she said and licked her lips.

"That's all your fault." He quickly pulled open the towel that was covering her. "And you're all wet now, so I'm going to have to dry you off as well."

He dabbed and stroked her breasts dry with the soft Egyptian cotton towel, ignoring her small cries of protest as he buffed her nipples gently into stiff peaks again. He kissed her and then went to work between her legs. The friction of the thick fabric was hugely erotic as he rhythmically stroked it backwards and forwards igniting the nerve endings of her sex until she couldn't stand it much longer. "Let me touch you now," she pleaded and reached towards him.

"No," he said softly. "It's all about you this time. I want to make you feel amazing. Indulge your fantasies. Tell me exactly what you want me to do and I will."

Helen closed her eyes and shivered as his mouth brushed over her breast and the towel slid back and forth. "Anything?"

"Anything."

She heard his breath stall as he watched her fingers trail to her other breast and start to stroke. "I'd like to watch you."

"Watch me?"

"Yes."

"You mean—"

"You know what I mean," she said huskily. "Like when you're on your own."

"Naughty girl," he said as she flipped onto her side and patted the bed.

She couldn't believe she was doing it, suggesting he do *that*, but she could push the limits as far as he could. Maybe further. "Come on," she whispered. "If you want to…"

He'd been hot, hard and ready ever since they'd got under the shower and her spine felt as if it was melting as he began. He closed his eyes, long lashes black against the smooth bronze of his skin and his lips parted slightly. She dared not blink as she watched his fingers, long and slender with square tips, and her breasts ached as they curled around and started to move.

He was beautiful and the scene unfolding in front of her was taboo, but he was letting her watch it, letting her into his secret world. The silence intensified her arousal. No talking or touching allowed as his rhythm became steady. Long, slow strokes just like with the bath towel and the shower gel. His mouth opened wider and she willed him to make a noise, but he didn't, just his breath growing harsher and more feverish. His chest and shoulders grew tense, his movements more jerky, and she could stand it no more.

"Condom," she muttered and put her hand over his to stall him. His eyelids opened with surprise, large black pupils circled with gold. "Now."

"Top drawer." She leant over him, and as she grabbed the handle he took a nipple into his mouth and sucked hard. He held her there for a few seconds and then bit down gently until she quivered. He let her breast drop free. "I should say no to you after what you just made me do."

"Say no and I will have to kill you," she gasped as she fumbled with the protection. "Christ, how do you ever get this thing open."

"It's a skill." He snatched it from her fingers. "Now kiss me."

She heard the condom rustle and then snap into place as her tongue tangled with his, and then felt the thick head of him pushing upwards against her entrance. She groaned against his lips as his hands came around her hips and pressed her buttocks up the length of his body and down until she was impaled with half his length. "Christ…"

"Too much for you, mistress?" He flexed his hips and pulled her down further, his eyes now flashing dangerously. "Can't take what you hand out?"

"I can take it." She moaned deeply as she braced her hands on his chest and took him all in. Stretched wide and deep, the sensation of him forced tight against the neck of her womb was intoxicating. Her breasts trembled as she tentatively began to ride him. "I can take everything you've got."

"Then do it quickly." He closed his eyes, the muscles of his neck straining as she slid back and forth, teasing his mouth with her nipples as her breasts swung against his face.

She closed her own eyes, reveling in the hedonism of their act, the feel of his balls tightening against her bottom and then his fingers dipping between them. "No," she said as he flicked mercilessly beneath the soft hood of her clitoris. "Not yet."

"Yes," he said in a harsh voice, and thrust his hips upwards and increased the friction, exciting every inch of her until she began to tip over the edge.

She cried out as she arched her back, pressing into his hand and down hard on his huge penis. The image of him masturbating flashed into her mind as she felt him flex deliberately inside her, igniting the nerve endings at the front side of her vagina and making her gasp with the agony of it. She heard him cry out as his orgasm began, and the primal sound of him mating with her was too much for her to hold back any longer. Her body was strung tight with a thrilling pleasure she would never be able to forget or deny herself again, and she tumbled helplessly into a blazing ecstasy of mutual climax.

Chapter Ten

"What do you think of our day out so far?"

Relaxing in the shade of a cool vine-covered restaurant terrace, Helen lifted her sunglasses and propped them on top of her head. He'd promised at breakfast to bring her somewhere she'd simply love that morning, and she hadn't been disappointed. Her first sightseeing tour of the island had been exhilarating and now she was looking forward to a good lunch. "It's been fabulous, although I must say the drive up that mountain was pretty hair raising."

"Monte Toro?" Ricardo laughed and his eyes twinkled with mischief. "It's only the highest mountain in Menorca."

"Yes, so you said as I was cowering with fear on the way up! A mere three hundred and fifty seven meters, wasn't it?"

"Well remembered. But you did get to see the entire island from up there, so you mustn't complain."

"Not complaining. Very impressed. You even arranged for it to be a beautifully cloud free day."

He feigned a cough. "And the breeze helped blow the last of Tino's smoke out of our lungs."

"Good job too. You snored last night…"

"I shall ignore that. Now what would you like to drink. Beer? Wine? It's a limited tariff but all sourced from around here, local and very good."

"White wine would be nice." Helen ran her fingers over the scrolled edge of the table and picked up a white plastic covered menu. She turned it over in her hands curiously. "This is an intriguing place, you'd never know it was here. No sign outside, tucked away in a side street through a low archway. I thought it was someone's house."

"It *is* someone's house. Antonio's house. It's not listed anywhere, doesn't need to be. His reputation as a chef is legendary on the island, one of our best kept secrets." Ricardo winked. "He doesn't speak a word of English, and if Antonio doesn't like the look of you, you won't be served. So best behavior, please."

Helen formed her mouth into a silent O and resisted the naughty urge to poke her tongue out. As Ricardo disappeared through an archway into the dark and mysterious interior of the old town house she looked around the empty terrace full of neatly set tables. They must be the first customers of the day. She certainly hadn't been expecting this gem in the middle of nowhere. The little town at the foot of the mountain was unremarkable, but quaint and pleasant, off the tourist trail, though, if Ricardo's description of it was accurate. The former hometown of a notorious gangster, where sunbathing and mini-skirts were frowned upon. *So* not like Ibiza and Marbella.

Ricardo returned, carrying an ice bucket in one hand and two large, chilled glasses in the other. Helen watched him approach, the fabric of his white shirt stretching over hard knots of bicep as he moved. Just looking at him made her heart beat faster, and those long, muscular legs and narrow hips in black chinos made her mouth feel suddenly dry. The man was driving her to drink.

"I hope you don't mind, but Antonio insists on preparing us a selection of today's specialties." Ricardo filled their glasses from the condensation-beaded wine bottle. "I don't think we'll be disappointed."

"I'm not going to question Antonio after what you've told me. I'm hungry and don't want to find myself out on my ear." She took a sip of the golden liquid and shivered with pleasure as its sweet freshness trickled down her throat. "Although I'm really going to have to start easing up on the food out here. Lucia's pastries every morning are bound to start taking a toll."

"I forbid you to even think about going on a stupid diet," Ricardo said sternly. "Not only do we have some of the best food in the world here, but I have plenty of money to pay for it out here in the sunshine. So enjoy it all while you can. In three months you can go running back to your baked beans or whatever you normally eat in the rain in England, and all this will be a distant memory."

Helen appreciated the sentiment. Her nose suddenly picked up some intensely savory aromas. "Baked beans? Black cabbage, if you don't mind. And a vast assortment of root vegetables."

"Exactly." Ricardo folded his hands into a tepee shape and rested his chin on the points of his fingers. A small smile flickered across his lips as a young boy arrived with a wooden serving trolley. "Besides, I can't think how you're possibly going to be able to resist any of this."

"You may well have a point." Helen felt her mouth begin to water as she scanned the delicacies being placed on the table in front of them.

The shy-looking boy gestured towards a steaming bowl of gondola-shaped pasta with scampi, rocket and cherry tomatoes, *cortecce*, and then swept his long, thin arm grandly towards the second. "*E benfatti*."

Helen closed her eyes for a second and breathed in the unctuous steam coming from the plates. "Oh my God, they both smell amazing. Which one's mine?"

"We're starry-eyed lovers. We share."

"Thank God I don't have to make a decision." Helen eyed the shiny pile of creamy linguine hungrily and breathed in the delicious aroma.

"Smoked Monte Toro goat's cheese, honey mushrooms, and basil from the back garden," Ricardo said, as if he had been reading her mind.

"So you really *have* been here before," she said and adjusted her cutlery as Ricardo served them a large helping of each dish.

"Of course," he said with a crooked smile. "I know that all the pasta is freshly made by Antonio's Italian wife and daughters. If you pop inside later, you'll see them making it on a great big wooden table in the hall. It's cool in there, so nothing dries out too quickly."

The boy scuttled off at the sound of a woman's raised voice from indoors, and Helen took her first bite of food. The *benfatti* melted in her mouth and left a lingering tang of pungent wood smoke on her palate. It would be impossible not to eat the lot.

"Good?" Ricardo speared a dark, silken mushroom with his fork.

"Unbelievable." Helen closed her eyes in reverence to the sweetest shellfish she had ever eaten. The flavors burst on her palate and sung of the sea and the pine forests. "I'm going to be the size of a semi-detached house in three months at this rate."

"Just make sure you make a fuss of Antonio when he

comes out." Ricardo chuckled. "He responds very well to praise, and he's a devil when it comes to the ladies."

Helen shot him a cheeky look. "Aren't you all?"

"Some worse than others." He tore open a crusty bread roll. "And I'll go to extraordinary lengths to get a reduction on the bill, so lay it on thick."

Helen giggled as she examined the pea-pod shaped piece of pasta on the end of her fork. "This is lovely." She bit slowly and thoughtfully on to the saucy morsel. "I've quite a long-standing interest in pasta, actually, so I'd really like to visit the kitchen later, if I may."

"I'm fascinated," Ricardo said sardonically. "I thought pasta only came in tins in the UK."

"Ignoramus." Helen frowned at him. "There's durum wheat growing not far from our house I'll have you know."

The young boy returned to collect their plates that had been wiped clean with pieces of rustic bread.

"Don't rush off, Pirro," Ricardo said in Spanish. "Say hi to Helen. She won't bite."

Pirro's foal-like eyes flickered from Ricardo to Helen and back again. Then a shy smile spread across his face.

"How's school these days?" Ricardo winked at him. "Still turning up for your lessons, I hope?"

Pirro nodded and his black hair trembled endearingly as he took the empty plates and put them on the bottom shelf of the trolley. "Papa got me a bike, so I can ride like the wind down the back lane, *Tio Ricardo.*"

Ricardo eyes widened with drama. "And back up it again?"

Pirro giggled and sneaked a quick glance at Helen. "Sometimes, but I usually cheat. Senor Garcia lets me hop on his bus when no one's checking, just as long as I remember to bring him one of Mama's cakes for his afternoon coffee."

Ricardo laughed and ruffled the boy's head until he squeaked with protest. "Lazy toad! Let's hope all that soccer practice is keeping you in shape, then!"

Pirro puffed out his chest like an opera singer. "I am team captain, Ricardo," he said proudly. "I told you I'd make it!"

"Good lad! I knew all that hard work would pay off. Bravo!"

Helen watched as the man and the boy became ever more animated, cuffing each other and joking like the old friends they obviously were, until a woman's voice called out for the third time. Impatience was creeping into her tone.

"You'd better scoot or Maria will be out to tell me off again," Ricardo said as he took the new steaming plates Pirro had uncovered on the trolley and was now quickly handing to him.

"Like a couple of weeks ago!" Pirro laughed over his shoulder as he trotted back towards the kitchen.

Helen propped her chin on her hands and watched as Ricardo served them both from two enormous platters. One was filled with a plait of white fish on fried potatoes, scattered with walnuts and rosemary oil. The second was a fillet of pork on what looked like cottage cheese, drizzled with a sage cream.

"Wow! Things just get better and better."

"I'm glad you're impressed," Ricardo said as he piled up their plates. "So tell me about Ibiza. What were you doing in town before Antonella got her shiny claws into you?"

"A short-term contract in a salt company's office. They needed translation support done on some promotional material. I think I managed to get in because my Spanish and computer skills are passable, and I was in the right place at the right time."

"So you said your contract was terminated. A bad girl,

were you?"

"You wish. No. Financial problems somewhere along the line, apparently. The office needed to be relocated to the mainland, that's all I was told. Along with *adios*."

"It happens," Ricardo murmured as he concentrated on his food. "How many languages do you speak? Spanish, Mandarin, Russian…"

"A bit of Italian, French and a few words of German."

"Quite the achiever! It sounds like your talents were wasted in the Ibiza salt mines anyway." Helen flicked away an insect. "It sounds impressive, but my degree was in Spanish, French, and Agriculture. The rest are what I've picked up on the side, just for the fun of it. There's very little money in it, but languages come easily to me. Mum says I must have been a parrot in a previous life." She shrugged and opened her eyes deliberately wide. "See? I'm chattering on and boring you silly without even trying."

"On the contrary. I'm fascinated."

He shot her a suggestive look and she couldn't be sure if he was being sarcastic or if he really meant what he'd said, but either way her mind had now melted into jelly. "So you must come to this restaurant often?"

He smiled. "Yes, as often as I can. The food is excellent, no one is nosy or sticking a camera in my face. It's like being Mr. Average Anonymous for once. Sometimes there are definite downsides to being rich, influential and, dare I say it, an Almanza."

"It must be difficult guarding your privacy."

Ricardo stared into his wine for a moment. "I also like to visit often to keep an eye on Pirro. Poor kid had a really tough start in life. I've known him since the beginning. But Antonio and Maria have brought him up well—fresh air, freedom and honest work. The odd clip around the ear too, I expect."

"Never did you any harm, eh?" Helen said, her composure returning.

"Sadly not. My papa was never around long enough to deliver the discipline. He'd always be back from business with gifts and kisses. Mama used to get very angry. But of course, we adored him for all that indulgence. He was more of a grandfather figure than a dad, I suppose. It was great at the time, but—" He thoughtfully ran a finger up the stem of his glass. "I don't think it did us much good in the long run. Having to accept the word no is one of life's hardest lessons. I still don't like it."

"I could make a sarcastic remark, but I won't."

Ricardo began to laugh as Pirro arrived with their desserts. "Got a girlfriend yet?" he asked as the boy put down the glass dishes.

Pirro giggled and a color rose on his shiny round cheeks. "Not yet, Ricardo, but…" He leant to whisper something in Ricardo's ear while pretending to rearrange the cutlery, until Ricardo sent him packing back off to the kitchen whooping with laughter.

Helen's eyebrows rose questioningly.

"He said he likes the look of *my* girlfriend."

"Serves you right."

"For what, exactly?"

"For being such a dreadful man." She took a spoonful of *turrón* ice cream and grinned. "Although you do seem a lot more relaxed and cheerful in Menorca. Or is that my imagination?"

"It's the wine, *querida*," he said with a lethal grin and refilled her glass. "So let's have some more."

Helen watched appreciatively as the wine bubbled into her glass, sparkling with hints of lime green in the sunshine. "Thank you."

"I think you're pretty nice all the time," he said quietly before scooping cinnamon mousse onto a sweet wafer biscuit. "Now that you've stopped snarling at me, that is."

"Have I ever done that?" Helen replied cautiously. "Snarled at you?"

He gave her a serious look "It's felt like it at times, considering we're just helping each other out."

"Then I apologize."

"No need. I probably deserved it anyway." He wiped his fingers on a napkin and then scraped back his chair. "I'll get these back to the kitchen and see how my other favorite ladies are getting on. I won't be long."

She watched as he walked back towards the house, dishes in hand, his dark head held high. Every movement he made sent bolts of awareness shooting through her. She shivered with the delicious sensation. No man had a right to be so damn attractive.

She saw a gray-haired woman in the shadows of the main building entrance, presumably Maria, wipe her hands on a blue-and-white-striped apron. Ricardo bent down to kiss the top of her head and her short, shaky forearms reached up to cup his face. He submitted totally as the old lady fussed over his clothes, his hair, and if Helen wasn't mistaken, she could hear Maria berate him for being too skinny and in need of a decent wife to feed him up.

After a few minutes, Ricardo sauntered back towards Helen carrying coffee and briefly looked back over his shoulder. Maria and three young women were peering around the white stone doorway and giggled as they waved in Helen's direction. Turning his attention back to her, his smile widened.

"I told them. I hope you don't mind, I just couldn't help myself," he whispered.

"Told them what?"

Ricardo leaned across the table and covered Helen's tiny hand with his. "That we got married."

Helen winced. "Ah, that. They didn't know? Are they angry with you? I'll bet they *hate* me!"

"Not a bit of it. They had no idea about us, no interest in celebrity gossip outside the village, but they're ecstatic. Maria wants to bake us a special cake."

"I hope you didn't tell her I could cook."

"The subject never arose. They're all just happy I've finally found someone."

Helen felt herself being drawn into the amber fire of his eyes, and her heart skittered dramatically for a few seconds as his words sank in. She *was* married to this incredibly attractive, totally masculine, virile male. He was perfect husband material on the surface — older, wiser, stronger, and unapologetically dominant. She knew she should will away the sudden and irrational longing for their marriage to be real. She'd felt that way before, and knew it was dangerous.

Her voice sounded husky. "Finally found someone? Someone like me?"

"Why not? In another time, another place and in different circumstances it might have happened anyway."

"*It*?"

He smiled and looked down into his coffee cup as it swirled around a silver spoon. "Us."

"Highly unlikely, we live in different worlds. And, besides, you said the last thing you ever wanted to do was to get married."

"So did you."

A burst of sadness made her feel weak. The cold truth had intruded on their intimacy. The words tumbled from her mouth before she could stop them, an attempt to build a wall around her heart. "And I still feel the same."

"Are you sure?"

I'm sure I want to go straight home, back into bed with you. Sure, I want to feel the hot weight of your body on mine. Sure, I'd have your babies if you wanted me to because…I'm falling in love with you.

She pasted on a false smile. "Of course I'm sure."

She was shocked at the way her mind had rambled into forbidden territory. It had to be the wine, the sultry atmosphere…or just Ricardo and the lust he invoked. Torturous heat intensified between her tightly clamped thighs. He could suggest anything to her at that moment, and she would agree. She wanted him so badly again it hurt.

Ricardo had never needed to pay her the extra million. He was destined to have her anyway. From that very first moment, as he stared down at her spread-eagled on the Condesa's bed. The flashing citrine and jet of his eyes had made her heart stall. The sensuous curve of his lips, the angry flare of his nostrils, and the intense power of his hands at her throat were instantly thrilling. She'd been ready to submit to him there and then, within a minute of their worlds colliding. Facing up to the naked truth about how she felt about this man was deeply disturbing.

She realized she was under his spell.

Chapter Eleven

"Do you remember the day we met?" Helen asked later, as they stood on the balcony of his bedroom, watching the sunset after another perfect honeymoon day.

"How could I possibly forget?" he murmured into her hair, his arms winding around her slim waist as he stood behind her. "You were like a trapped animal in that room. An animal with a very attractive behind."

"Even in my horrible work pants?"

"I've ripped them off in my fantasies many times, don't you worry"

"You've had fantasies about me?"

His hand slid up from her waist and began to stroke her breast through the fine silk of her bathrobe. "Of course I have. I still do when you're not here to indulge me for real."

The thought of him fantasizing about her was an instant turn on. An image flashed through her mind of him lying naked on his bed, his hand resting on his flat stomach and then... Her voice was suddenly low and sexy. She liked the sound of that too. "I remember the feel of your knees on the back of mine as you pushed me down. I thought you were going to—"

"Murder you?"

"Possibly, or…*have* me."

"You weren't particularly receptive that day. You almost crippled me in that department."

She heard him take a long, slow breath and reach for her other breast. She pictured him closing his eyes as he felt her, as he cupped her curves and molded them against his large hands. She loved that he wanted to enjoy her. "In your fantasy, do you take me there on the bed? From behind?"

His fingers grew still and she could feel his heartbeat between her shoulder blades. "Sometimes."

"Is it…is it primitive? Rough?" His hands began to move lightly across her breasts again. He must be able to feel the way her heartbeat had increased with excitement.

"No, it's exquisite because you beg me to do it to you."

Helen gripped the cold stone shelf of the balcony as she felt his growing erection pressing through the sheer material covering her bottom. His own robe was never going to restrain him, that part of him was too powerful for Chinese silk. "And do you? Do you do it to me when I beg you?"

"Always." Ricardo trailed one hand up the length of her thigh, twisting her robe in his hand and lifting it up and around her waist to expose her naked lower half. "You're always ready for me, very eager, very wet, and I'm always prepared…"

Helen heard him tear open a condom wrapper with his teeth and instinctively leaned her weight forward against the stone balustrade. He was going to…and she wanted him to so badly. The hard, cold balcony pushed against her rib cage beneath her breasts and she roughly pulled the edges of the robe apart to intensify the sensation, letting it slide off her shoulders, his penis was hot and rigid as it slid between her parted thighs and the cool night breeze tightened her nipples. He nudged along her vulva with his length, back and forth until she began to groan. "Yes…please. Now."

She heard him adjust his footing as her robe slid to the floor and she felt the immediate pressure of him pushing upwards and into her. His thickness stretching her wide, the weight of him against her back and buttocks pressing, back and forth in tiny movements until one long thrust secured him deep inside. His voice was low and hoarse. "I've wanted you like this for so long."

She gasped with excitement as he reached around and slid his fingers between her legs, stroking, exploring until he found her swollen nub and began to tease her senseless with his fingertips. Tiny circles that made her bones melt and a sharp flick to heighten the pleasure as he thrust hard into her. "Ricardo…yes…more…"

She heard his breathing grow harsh as she pushed back against him, begging him with her body to go further and faster. She felt his hands slide to her hips and grip her firmly in place, his lips and body hair rasping against her bareback. "Can you feel it, *querida*? Can you feel how much I want you?"

He was huge inside her and she felt wilder and more sensual than she ever had before. He was irresistible. "I want it all," she moaned. Her feet lifted slightly from the cold tiled floor as she spread her legs as wide as possible and she felt his fingertips dig into the soft flesh on her hips.

"On your knees then," he whispered harshly against her neck and pressed against her until her nipples were flattened against the stone balcony. "On the lounger."

Helen looked to her left and knew exactly what he had in mind. It was perfect, deep and wide cream cushions just inches away. He turned her around, his thick shaft still inside her and the twisting sensation it caused in her vagina made her shiver. She was already close to the edge. He eased her forward against the lounger so that her knees touched the fabric and her words seemed to come from nowhere. "Push me down." The breath left her body and she twisted her face to the side as his weight came slowly down. Blind lust ripped through her as her breasts were crushed against the coarse cotton fabric, stiff nipples inverting with the pressure and buzzing with intense arousal. "Now *have* me."

"Lift up for me," Ricardo muttered as the fingers of one hand found her clitoris again. "So I can go really deep, make you come really hard."

Every muscle in her body was tight with anticipation as she curved her back and offered herself up to him as far as she could. His fingers circled her hot flesh as he began to move, each sliding movement pushing her breasts upwards and into the rough fibers of the cushion until his other hand slid beneath her and sought out a hard nipple. He nipped it firmly and repeatedly between his fingers until her hips bucked in reflex, then she cried out as he gently pinched her clitoris at the same time. "Oh God…"

"That's it," his voice trembled slightly as his pace increased. Long powerful thrusts that brought his balls in tightly so their pubic hair meshed and increased the friction between their bodies.

Within seconds she began to tumble helplessly into orgasm, delirious with black hot sensation as his penis took control of her entire body. Plunging, panting, her fingers clawed the cushion and she didn't care who heard her scream as she started to climax.

Ricardo groaned loudly as his own release became imminent and his rhythm changed. Drops of his sweat felt cold as they landed on the hot skin of her back and shoulders.

What he was doing to her felt savage and she welcomed it, she wanted it. She ached for him to totally possess her in that moment of heat and musk and feral need. She heard him curse in Catalan, dark sentences that included her name and then a brief moment of breathless silence as his body went into spasm and she felt him start to come. His body shuddered his release into her, long and slow, and he made a low noise that sounded almost like he was in pain. She felt her vagina close around him, convulse, twist and squeeze until she too tipped over the edge into her own swirling abyss of orgasm.

He had her.

There was no going back. Body, soul, and heart, she was his.

• • •

Ricardo awoke with a start. She was there with him, in his bed, soft and warm. He looked down and saw she was still out for the count with her nose pressed against his chest. It was a cute nose. He listened to her breathing, slow and regular and wondered if he really *did* snore. Nobody had ever mentioned it before.

He rubbed his eyes with the hand that wasn't pinned to the bed by the woman and realized that he hadn't slept with many of his consorts. He'd had sex with plenty, but he usually found a way to avoid seeing them in the morning. There was something about "morning" that was far too intimate for his liking, far too much like the beginning of something meaningful.

He should get up, extricate himself quietly and shower. He should…Ricardo closed his eyes and inhaled her scent, the sweet herbs of her shampoo still lingered and his pillow felt more comfortable than he could ever remember. He'd been sleeping a lot more soundly since Helen had been sharing his bed and knew he shouldn't get used to it, but still he couldn't bear to get up and leave her there sleeping. He felt safe there.

His thoughts drifted to her parents in their ramshackle farmhouse full of cobwebs and kittens. They had very little in a material sense, but they had each other and that seemed to be enough for them. He supposed they'd say they loved each other as husband and wife should. Maybe it was possible to find happiness within a marriage. Maybe some marriages did last. Maybe some lucky people really did go on to find a "Happy Ever After," but that didn't mean he'd started to believe in love.

The simple comfort of their marriage bed and having time to lie there and think was beginning to lull him into exploring dangerous ideas, like ideas about families, the stuff normal people did. Perhaps it wouldn't be so bad...

He looked down at her again, at his wife, and felt a pang of anxiety. She was there because she loved money, not because she had any feelings for him, and he shouldn't forget that. But then again, if that was her only fault he could deal with it. He had more than enough money to keep a small country running, and, quite frankly, most women wanted rich husbands, didn't they? It was biological, an instinct to find the best mate to father their offspring. He wouldn't want to become suddenly penniless, either, if he was honest, and what were the chances of him ever finding a woman who wasn't interested in his wealth? Zero.

"Ricardo?" she murmured, and he felt her begin to stir.

"I'm here, honey, go back to sleep." He tried not to panic at the way his stomach had flipped at the sound of her voice. His heart was already beginning to race as he felt her fingers trace sleepy circles on his chest. He swallowed hard when he realized he'd just made a huge life-changing decision without hesitation.

"You're beautiful," she said, eyes closed, still half asleep.

"So are you." He squeezed his eyes tightly shut. He wanted to keep her. He wanted her to stay his wife.

He needed a plan.

Chapter Twelve

Helen's hand trailed over the side door of Ricardo's old red Alfa Romeo Spider, feeling the wind blast through her fingers as the car sped uphill. He had a collection of cars tucked away in a huge barn on the estate and had insisted she choose which one they took out for the day. The breeze became refreshingly cool in the summer heat as they gained altitude and he negotiated the rough mountainous road.

Helen giggled as they bumped over the ridges and potholes. "This is loads more fun than your uptight Ferrari!" she shouted over the noise of the engine and crunching of the road beneath the wheels.

"Papa would have been delighted to hear that!" he shouted back. "He bought her in the sixties and could never bear to upgrade." He shot her a grin as his black hair flew about in the wind. "She's been part of the place for a long time now, part of the family."

The car roared up a steep incline and Helen gasped as the dusty road suddenly ended and they ground to a halt at the very top. It must have been another of the highest points of the island, a huge expanse of sea and sky as far as the eyes could see.

"It's like being one of the gods up here, isn't it?" Ricardo said, opening the low car door for her to get out. "It's got to be the nearest place to heaven I've ever been."

Helen nodded with delight as he pulled out the basket of lunch items he had packed earlier and a large rolled up blanket for them to sit on.

"We can leave these here for a bit," Ricardo said putting the things down on the grass. "There's something I want to show you." He took her hand and helped her towards the edge of a cliff where a flight of wooden steps down appeared. Helen gripped his hand tightly and he squeezed it reassuringly. The steps were very steep. The ground eventually leveled off and he guided her onto a large semi-circle carved into the rock of the cliff. There was no barrier or fence, and the wind was whipping the dark blue sea into white-capped peaks hundreds of feet below them. It didn't feel particularly safe, and Helen's fingers instinctively tightened around his shirtsleeve.

"As I'm only going to be married the once," Ricardo said, gesturing to their left, "I thought I'd better present you to the family."

Helen's mouth fell open as her eyes focused upon what was unmistakably a mausoleum. "Oh…"

"I hope you don't think I'm weird," Ricardo said quickly. "I always make a point of coming up here as soon as I can when I'm staying at Dizzy Heights. It's one of the first things I do, a ritual."

"That's okay," Helen whispered and took a step forward to read the bold black lettering carved into the tomb. "We should have brought some flowers."

"It's pretty enough without flowers. They'd just blow away on a day like this. Besides, I don't think anything can compete with the view from here, do you?" Ricardo closed his eyes and breathed in the sea air. "Our parents brought us here every summer for picnics. It was their favorite place. I don't know if it's true or not, but Lucia says that this is where Dad proposed to our mom all those years ago." He looked at Helen with a sudden softness in his eyes. "The Alfa's the only car that's ever been up here too."

"It's a very special place," Helen said, a lump forming in her throat. "You must always keep it this way." She traced her fingers over the stonework. "Alegria Cadelaria Almanza. A beautiful name." Ricardo nodded. "Primeiro Salbatore Almanza. Your brother?"

Helen saw the quick movement of his Adams apple as he swallowed and looked away. "My twin brother."

"And Ricardo Primeiro Almanza must be your father…"

"Yes." Helen could sense that his mood was altering. Enough was enough. "Let's go back now, get out of this wind," he said and took her firmly by the hand.

They trudged back up in silence, just the sound of their feet and breath and the whistling gale. They reached the plateau above and made their way inland towards the car through the long grass and wild flowers. The air became warmer as the breeze dropped.

"So how do you like being Mrs. Almanza so far?" Ricardo said as he sat down beside Helen on the blanket.

"It could be a lot worse." She flicked off a sandal and ran the inside of her foot up his calf muscle. "You feed me, don't you?"

He brushed an unruly windswept lock of hair out of her eyes. "Almost constantly, it seems."

"Like a baby cuckoo?" she said guardedly, remembering the term he'd used to describe her to the Condesa on that first day.

Ricardo started to empty the basket's contents onto the

picnic blanket and avoided her eyes. "You have a very long memory and large ears for someone so young."

"Like a baby elephant, then?" Helen giggled and then noticed he was suddenly agitated, fussing over cutting them some bread. He'd just ripped a piece off and given it to her before now. "Are you okay?"

He pinned her with a stare that gave nothing away. "Of course, why shouldn't I be?"

Because you've just visited the grave of your entire family?

How could he hide the emotion he must be feeling? She clamped her jaw together for a moment to steady her voice. Perhaps also to hold back the words that were on the tip of her tongue, but they came out anyway. "How do you do it?"

"Do what?"

"How you can be so emotionally cold one minute and the Spanish superhero the next? I can't work you out. You're unfathomable. You say you don't want marriage, for example, but it flies totally in the face of the way you live your life, the people who surround and love you. Marriage and family life is so traditional, respectable, solid. It doesn't fit."

"Because I haven't been able to trust anyone like that for a long time." He said softly and looked up at her at last, his gaze tinged with pain. "Do you want to hear my experience of marriage, Helen? All the gory details? The reasons why I'd never have considered it unless I had to?"

Helen felt nervous, but she had to hear this. "Go on."

"My father cheated on Mama habitually. It was part of normal life for them. He was always away on 'business' and he was careful to be discreet, but none of it seemed to shame him at all, breaking the vows he'd made in church, cheating on the woman that loved him. So it came as no surprise when Mama started doing the same thing. She was desperate for love and affection. She had to go outside their marriage to find it." He snatched at the grass irritably. "Maybe I'm being too harsh, but I see the whole marriage thing as a pointless after that."

"It must have been hard," Helen said quietly. "I can't imagine my parents ever behaving that way."

"So there's my parents' dreadful marriage, but if you really want to understand what makes me so cold, think back to the family tomb down there, will you? Do you remember anything unusual about it?"

Helen's eyes flickered helplessly across his face for clues. She'd seen the three names, but as for anything else…

"Let me help you. The dates." Ricardo's jet eyebrows rose questioningly. "Mama and Primeiro?"

Helen shook her head in defeat.

"They died on the same day."

Helen's eyes fell to her lap and she fiddled nervously with the hem of her blouse. This had to be bad. "What happened to them?"

Ricardo ground his jaw for a moment, and Helen didn't think she was going to get an answer. He leaned back on one elbow. "Cold blooded murder," he muttered. "They were both shot. Mama died instantly. She was dead when I got there. Primeiro bled to death in my arms before the services could arrive. I tried to save him, but it was a major artery and his brain was just…"

Helens hand flew to her mouth in shock. "Who did it?"

"His *wife*. She'd sworn she was off the drink and drugs before they married. The *perra* lied. Primeiro was generous with his money and so busy with his work he never noticed a thing. God, that woman must have been born devious."

Helen held her hands against her hot cheeks. "That's awful."

"Anyway, she got lazy in her habits and was found out. Primeiro wanted a divorce and her out of his life. He set the lawyers to work immediately. Mama went round to give him some moral support as soon as she found out. She never did like her. I wouldn't be surprised if she'd only gone round to gloat and change the locks personally, if I'm honest."

"Sometimes mothers have a sixth sense about these things."

"The toxicology report said Arabella had been drinking and had taken some heroin adulterated with some household chemical. Her brain was fried, hallucinating probably. She shot them both before throwing herself off their penthouse balcony. Or that's what they say. It was a mess."

Helen closed her eyes and smothered a sharp cry.

"It was up to me to tell Dad," Ricardo said quietly. He was in prison when it happened. He never forgave himself for not being there for them. As if he could have prevented it anyway. That's what finished him off, I think, a broken heart and shattered pride. I'll never forget the look on his face when I finally managed to get the words out. It still sickens me. Three days later he had a massive heart attack and died. So, I brought them all here. It seemed right. An unsullied place…"

"I don't know what to say." Helen reached out a hand to touch him.

"That's why Jerardo wanted to force me to marry, to do something I had no respect for as revenge for what my father took from him. He tapped into the fact that I must be a total misogynist. Perhaps he's right. My mother was a cheat, my sister-in-law was a liar and a murderer, both of them unfazed by the holy state of matrimony. I've even had girlfriends who went through my wallet and helped themselves when I wasn't looking, you know. They didn't need to. If they'd only asked…"

"Not every woman's like that," Helen whispered, suddenly realizing that she must be on the end of a very long list of avaricious females.

"There are some good women in my life, you've met them. Even Antonella has her moments. She's vacuous, selfish, and spoiled, but to her credit she never cheated on my dad. She's even quite nice to me at times." He shrugged and threw a blade of grass into the air, watching as it twisted and sailed off in the breeze. "Or perhaps it's because I'm a trustee of her future funds."

"Really?"

"My father stipulated she could have whatever the Almanza fund deemed necessary for a civilized life on condition that she never remarried or brought shame on the Almanza name. It's up to me and his old friend Antonio to decide what is *necessary* for her. She has lovers, I know that. They sneak in when the rest of the staff have been dismissed. And she sleeps with the staff when the house is quiet sometimes as well, but she's discreet, so I turn a blind eye. My father is dead and the poor cow's only human."

Helen was relieved that Ricardo knew what his stepmother got up to. She was wondering whether to tell him. "It really is complicated, isn't it?"

"And you say I'm cold? I'm not. I've had to become this way." His amber eyes searched hers and seemed to be pleading silently for something. "My father insisted that real men never cried. He never did and he expected the same of me, so I do my very best."

Helen fell silent. Her heart ached for Ricardo and his tragic loss and a large part of her now understood why he could be so unforgiving on the subject of love, marriage, and womankind. He was alone in the world, orphaned, save for the few trusted family friends she had met, beyond that it was a whirl of users, business associates and hangers on. No wonder he loved the honest simplicity and solitude of this island retreat and the mountains. They seemed to be the only places he was really at peace with himself.

"You told me you weren't into marriage either," Ricardo said suddenly. "But do you ever think about children? You women have a built in biological clock, don't you?"

Helen swallowed uncomfortably with surprise at this dramatic change of subject. Ricardo did seem to be in a peculiar mood. "Not that often. I have a decade or two left to worry about it. I'm not that old!"

"No, of course you're not," he said and passed her a bottle of fruit juice. "In principle, I mean, theoretically, in the future. One day."

"I don't suppose I'd want to die childless in the end, if that's what you mean." She screwed the lid off the bottle and took a swig before continuing. "Isn't that what it's all about? Why we're all here? To leave something behind us, something good?"

Ricardo nodded and looked out to sea, now twiddling a picked daisy between his fingers, the bread discarded and forgotten. "It's the natural course of things, I guess, the expected route to immortality."

What was he up to? Why these strange questions? She wasn't going to let it go now. "So what about you? You talk about getting the family property back for future generations, that's got to require an heir at some stage." Helen held her breath as she waited for his answer. Could it possibly be that he was going to suggest that she, that they, that together they might…

"Not at all. There already is one."

"There is?" Helen heard her breath catch as a chill ripped through her.

Ricardo's expression darkened and he looked away. "I'm sorry, I shouldn't have mentioned it. Forget I said anything."

"I can't. Tell me about him. Or is it a her?"

"I can't talk about that, I wanted to talk about—"

"Don't you dare brush me off like that! I insist you tell me."

"It has to be a secret until he's eighteen. There are other people involved. It's complicated."

"I'll bet it is!" Helen was dismayed to hear a tremor in her voice. She couldn't hide the emotion rising within her. "I can keep another bloody secret, Ricardo. I'm good at that remember? Nobody's discovered I'm a sham wife yet."

"You must tell no one."

"I promise."

"Pirro, the boy at the restaurant."

"Pirro? But why is he in the middle of nowhere with Antonio? You said he was adopted."

"He is," he said digging a heel roughly into the grass. "It had to be done in the circumstances. I couldn't look after a small baby. No more questions now, I don't want to discuss it. I've already said too much."

Helen felt queasy with shock and galled with disappointment. Ricardo had a secret child. It was starting to make sense as she recalled their visit to Antonio's place. Ricardo's affection for the boy, his interest in school and sport... Oh God and the resemblance! How could she not have noticed that? They both had the same long limbs, dark features, hair, the smile.

"And his mother?" Helen's throat hurt as she forced the words out, unable to look at him.

"His mother was a crazy bitch and she's gone for good." He stared blankly out to sea before adding, "that's already more than you should know."

Helen's head was spinning as she tried to make sense of what she had been told. "Does Pirro know?"

Ricardo shook his head. "He was told his parents died in tragic circumstances and that they loved him very much. He will discover his true inheritance when he turns eighteen and has had a normal, loving childhood out of the limelight." He rubbed the back of his neck and closed his eyes. "It really is for the best."

Helen's scalp prickled with outrage for Pirro and disgust for Ricardo's lack of concern. Not to mention the lies. "Don't you think he'll be shocked when he finds out?"

"Probably. But he'll cope."

"Don't be surprised if he hates you." How on earth could she have deluded herself into thinking Ricardo might want to have a child with her? She'd completely lost her mind in this place. He had no intention of prolonging their arrangement beyond the three months. It was time to snap out of this lunacy once and for all. But anger made her keep going. "Didn't you ever *consider* having him live with you?"

"A child needs two parents. Antonella tried for a while and I did what I could, but neither of us knew what we were doing. And then when Papa died, she made it quite clear that it could only be a temporary measure. It was kinder to let him go with Antonio and Maria. We knew they could be trusted to give him a good life."

"I guess that's what you would describe as tough love," Helen replied bitterly. "So thoughtful of you."

Helen felt crushed. He walked away from his son. If he could coldly hand over his own flesh and blood, what hope did she ever have of finding a niche in his heart? Why did she ever think for one second that Ricardo would see her in an exceptional light? He must consider her the ultimate gold digger, the one who asked for more. The harpy who callously took him for millions! He would never view her with anything more than contempt, a *perra,* a bitch, just like his sister-in-law and Pirro's mother.

"Christ, it's just as well this marriage isn't real because I'd be having serious doubts about it already." Helen abruptly stood up, ignoring the look of surprise on Ricardo's face. Her voice shook as she stood on one leg to put on her sandals. "I'd like to go back now, Ricardo. I need to phone my Mum."

Chapter Thirteen

Ricardo cursed under his breath and kicked at Lucia's old pine chair outside the kitchen door. He felt a stab of shame as it tumbled backwards onto the stone floor, snapping a few tender herbs from a planter as it went. He was experiencing acute frustration since Helen had stormed in from the car and said she would be a while on the phone.

He'd had it all planned out—the romantic picnic, his family skeletons brought out into the open, and then the surprise proposal that they remain married. He'd been honest and exposed his inner self in a way he had never dared, and then he'd completely screwed it up. That's what you got for trying to be honest. He knew exactly when the mood had changed. Helen had been sweet at the tomb, which he had been worried about taking her to. Not exactly a hot date. He'd broached the subject of children and then he'd mentioned Pirro…

She was angry with him because he wouldn't tell her more about the circumstances of his adoption. But he couldn't. It was a stipulation in Primeiro's will, the child provision clause that insisted his child be brought up anonymously in the event of both parents' death. Out of the public eye until his eighteenth birthday when he would inherit and be old enough to make his own decisions.

He wanted to tell her how much it had hurt him to comply with those wishes, how it had torn his heart to shreds to hand over his twin brother's child.

He could tell her once she agreed to remain as his wife for real. Then, when he had that commitment from her, he would be sure that he could trust her to keep the Almanza secret that Pirro was the true heir who would always be a non-negotiable part of his life. He loved the boy as if he was his own. How could he not?

Then his heart stilled for a second. Maybe she would be disappointed that any child they had together would not be the Almanza empire's heir? He shook his head to erase the thought. Helen could never be that greedy, and besides he could provide her with more than she could ever dream of. The Almanza empire was vast, but Ricardo had made as many, if not more, millions in his own right. He *was* a self-made billionaire after all.

The issue niggled at him. He needed to know where those two million euro he'd given Helen had gone if they were to remain as man and wife in a proper sense. There had to be no other secrets between them. He'd already seen what deceit had done to his family and that poison was not going to leach into another generation if he had his way. He would have it out with her. Gently. Sensitively. And if all else failed he'd get his security people on to it, have her investigated, but that wouldn't be necessary, he was sure. He didn't want to do something like that behind her back unless he had to. If she was honest with him, and proved herself trustworthy he would tell her everything about him, everything she wanted to know.

• • •

"Bloody hell."

Helen flopped backwards onto the emperor-sized bed and covered her face with her hands. She'd lied to Ricardo about wanting to phone her mum. They'd already spoken that morning when Ricardo was getting the picnic ready and she was dressing. She just needed a few minutes to re-group, gather her thoughts and come to terms with the emotions muddling her brain. She had to deal with this rationally, logically, not hysterically, and she needed to form a business plan for her heart, just like she imagined Ricardo would. List out all the facts and form a strategy on the way forward.

Her hands dropped to her sides and she stared at the ceiling. "Stupid girl."

It wasn't just the great sex. It was hopeless whichever way she looked at it. However much her mind told her he was bad news, she loved him nevertheless. She had fallen in love with a man so cold he could give his own child away. But it had happened somewhere along the line without her even suspecting it was possible, and now she couldn't turn time back. She was angry with him, but couldn't alter the way she felt about him. She was stuck with it.

So what next? Her heart was going to be broken, that's what. In less than three months he would be out of her life forever and she'd be sent back into the world alone. What other options did she have? She should face the fact that Ricardo didn't want closeness or love. He didn't want a long-term relationship, and he'd hammered it home that he certainly didn't want a wife.

The best that could come out of this was for her to make the most of the time they had together, and for her to enjoy her honeymoon heaven while it lasted. It could be worse. She had plenty of money in the bank now so the world would be her oyster in the long future ahead. But she would never love again, not like this. No man would ever match up to Ricardo Almanza even with his deep flaws.

The bedroom phone began to ring and Helen bolted upright, feeling dizzy with the abruptness of her reaction. Instinctively, she picked up the receiver.

"Hello?"

"Darling, surprise! It's me, Antonella."

"Oh…hi." The sound of the Condesa's voice was an unwelcome one at the best of times, but this was supposed to be their honeymoon and her nerves were already in shreds. "Ricardo's not here right now. Shall I get him to call you back?"

"No, no, no, you silly girl. I'm on the internal line, in the drawing room. I've come to see you both. Isn't that fun?"

For God's sake.

"I'll be right down," Helen said, hoping the dread she was feeling didn't show in her voice. Hopefully she would just have to say a polite hello and Ricardo would deal with her from there. Lucia must have let her in and let Ricardo know his stepmother had turned up. "Just as quickly as I can."

It was naughty of her to dawdle, she knew that, but Helen had secretly hoped that the Condesa would get fidgety as usual and go off shopping or something before she came down. Five minutes was her usual boredom threshold. But no such luck. There she was, her black sky-high chignon poking up from behind the back of a large armchair. She turned upon hearing the door open. "Helen, how lovely to see you again. You look well…" Which meant 'you've put on weight.'

"And you, *Condesa*, are as radiant as always." Helen bent to kiss her politely on the cheek. "This *is* a surprise."

"You must call me Antonella now, dear, you're family after all." She smiled as if something amusing had occurred to her, and wriggled down comfortably into the cushions. "So where's my dreadful stepson?"

"I'm not actually sure," Helen said, feeling irritated that he wasn't there in body to deal with his unwelcome and uninvited relative. "I'd kind of assumed that he'd be here with you when you called."

"Some honeymoon," the Condesa hooted. "The bride's lost the groom already!"

God, the woman was annoying. "So, um, I'm assuming you got a cab up here? We're a fair way off the beaten track."

"Good grief, no! My new assistant's come away with me for a little break. I'm too exhausted for a cruise at this time of year, so she suggested a spot of island hopping. Great fun! And I thought that just so long as we're on Menorca, you could show her how you do the Bloody Marys." She ran her hands over her hairdo and did a theatrical shiver. "Wasn't that clever of me? I'm even multitasking now."

"A new assistant?" Helen was trying to summon up Ricardo with the power of thought alone and was failing miserably. Where *was* he? "That was quick work."

"I *know*! As luck would have it the agency had the perfect candidate, she'd just signed up, English like you. Except more refined."

"Right…" *Hell's teeth.* "So have you left the poor woman waiting for you in the car?"

"In the car? What do you think I am? Lou-lou? Lou-lou! Come here immediately and talk to Helen."

A distant female voice replied from outside on the terrace. "Coming, madam."

"Good, she's on her way." The Condesa made a harrumphing noise and heaved herself up and out of the armchair. "And *I'm* going to find that stupid boy, Ricardo. Have fun!"

Helen closed her eyes for a second to thank the universe that her Ordeal By Condesa was at an end. She listened to the sound of her heels clicking on the terracotta tiles until they faded away and then her blood froze.

"*Hola*, Mouse," the female voiced purred with pure poison. "It took me ages to track you down and find out the agency you worked for, but I got there in the end. Your mum was very obliging with info too, the gullible dip."

Helen's body stiffened as she took in the horribly familiar brown bob and harsh grey eyes. "What are you doing here, Kat? What do you want?" Her hands felt like blocks of ice as she gripped the back of a chair. "You can't get to me anymore."

"Darling!" the bully said briskly. "I can't imagine what you mean by that, and *do* call me Lidia, that's my name now, remember. Kat Humby is so common sounding now I've gone up so far in the world. Although, why that old bag insists on calling me *Lou-lou* is anyone's guess. Still, she's fulfilled her purpose now."

"I suppose I should be grateful you don't want us to call you by your ridiculous off the shelf title, *Lady* Skiptree."

"Oh, we're pretty much level pegging these days, Lovie. And that's part of the reason I wanted to pop in and congratulate you. I just *have* to know how you managed to bag that old devil Almanza. He swore he'd never do it, get married that is. You must have some spectacular tricks up your sleeve, darling, although God knows where you picked those up. It can't have been from your pony magazines, surely?" She snorted ungraciously and leant against the frame of the glass door. "He's damn fine in the sack, isn't he?"

"What are you talking about?" Helen felt a mixture of indignation and fear prickle over her.

"Oh, didn't he tell you? I suppose he's known hundreds of spectacular women in his time, so he may not have. We had a bit of a thing once, during a conference in London." The other woman barked a false laugh and took a step into the drawing room. "Isn't it just the most amazing coincidence? That he should end up marrying my old school chum? The chubby little girl that gave my brother her virginity in our barn."

Helen's mind went blank as she stood silently rubbing her brow. She couldn't think straight.

"Still awake, Mouse? I also thought you ought to know something else before Ricardo gets you to sign anything."

"Like what?" Helen knew her nemesis wasn't present through any good motive. She just wanted to run away, but knew it would be easier to hear her out than to have her dig her heels in and refuse to leave until she'd done what she'd set out to do.

"Please tell me you've not signed anything. You haven't, have you? He's very devious when it comes to business you know, you never get something for nothing with an Almanza, believe me."

"Just get on with it and get out."

"The marina development is a joint venture between the Skiptree Estate and Fothergill Enterprises."

"So?" Helen said. That deal was no secret, but where was Ricardo supposed to come in all this?

Lidia sighed heavily. "Oh Mousey Marshall, you're as dim and gullible as your mother. Fothergill is the UK operating subsidiary of the Almanza empire. They use it to gloss over the fact that prime land is being effectively developed by foreigners. Prevents some of the hippy protest nonsense at the planning application stage and lets us real business people get on with the business of making money. Have you worked it out yet? The development project is all Almanza's idea, his baby. Lock stock and barrel."

"You're making this up as you go along. Please stop being so spiteful and—"

Helen heard a sharp intake of breath as Lidia stepped closer and her voice dropped menacingly. "Who do you think pulled the plug on your parents' loan facility, darling? Anything to speed things up a bit. You don't keep Ricardo Almanza waiting, do you now? A teensy bit unethical on his part, but it did make me laugh at the time. What's the point in being the director of a world bank and not being able to pull a few strings, eh?"

"You really are an evil bitch."

"I'm concerned for you, mousy dear, in case he's trying to dupe you out of Primrose Farm as well. They have some peculiar laws out here when it comes to marriage and property. Mad Spaniards."

"I'm busy now, and I think it's time you and Antonella went on your way." Helen could feel her legs beginning to shake. "I'm assuming you took this job just to get to me, so that Bloody Mary recipe won't be necessary."

"You're smarter than you look. I'm sure you're eager to get back on your magnificent Spanish stallion, but I'm telling you it won't be long before he dumps you like all the others. Like he did me. And don't get any silly ideas about falling pregnant, waste of time financially. Rumor has it there's already an heir. Somewhere."

"Get out."

Lidia smiled and put her face so close to Helen's that she could smell her thick make up. "I'm finished with you for now anyway, Marshall, but you've not seen the last of me."

Helen heard her vile, poisonous laughter getting fainter as she slumped onto a sofa and felt sick. She scrunched her legs up tightly against her chest and rested her forehead on her knees.

How could she have been so completely and utterly stupid?

She would not cry. The bully would not make her cry again after all these years. Gritting her teeth and swallowing down the acidity in her throat, Helen knew she had to pull herself together. She couldn't let the bully win. Even though her chest began to feel uncomfortably tight, she walked calmly into the nearest bathroom, splashed water on her face, and applied some makeup to hide the signs of her distress. Her world was a mess and she had no idea what to do next, but whatever was going to happen, she might as well go and face it head on.

· · ·

"You must believe me. I had no idea that Antonella would pull a stunt like this," Ricardo said, pulling out a chair for Helen on the terrace. "I've given her a good telling off, and she'll be gone after she's had a swim and a shower."

"Thank goodness for that, because I was on the verge of killing her."

Ricardo chuckled. "And she honestly thought we'd believe the Bloody Mary thing? Talk about a ridiculous excuse for coming to have a good nose and get on our nerves."

"She did that all right."

"I didn't get to see her new slave though. She said she'd left her to chat with you? Any good?"

Now would be a good time to tell him what had happened, that she'd been tracked down and emotionally mauled by her oldest enemy, but there was no point now. He hadn't been there to protect her from it and he wouldn't be there the next time. And she was angry.

He blinked a few times waiting for an answer and soon

appeared to pick up on her hostility. His voice took on a business-like tone. "Was your Mum okay?"

"She's fine," Helen replied quietly, glad to have her sunglasses to hide behind.

"Good. So you feel better now?"

"I was until our visitors turned up." She took the glass of orange juice that he handed her, grateful he was oblivious to her fragile state of mind. "And after that I realized I'd lost my handbag. Must have left it up on the hill after the picnic. Could we go back for it?"

"Oh no!" He looked genuinely concerned. Either that or he was just pleased she wasn't beating him around the head with it. Her foul mood must be glaringly obvious. "But it'll be dark soon. I'm not sure we'd stand much chance of finding it tonight."

"Oh…"

"We'll get you a new one in the morning. It was an old thing anyway. Was there anything valuable in it? Your passport?"

"No, nothing like that."

"Sentimental value?"

"No."

"Then it can all be replaced. We'll do it tomorrow."

"Perhaps I could pop into Mahon on my own in the morning," she said quickly. "You won't have the first idea about what cosmetics I like and…ladies' stuff."

"We can go together."

Wretched man. "Aren't you busy?"

"Never too busy for you."

Helen exhaled slowly and calmly, hoping that the sea air would settle her. "Let's see what tomorrow brings."

"Good, that's settled then, because I need to talk to you about something."

He had nothing she wanted to hear. "I'm all ears."

"I'm not going to beat about the bush, Helen. I think we've grown quite close in the last few weeks, closer than I'd thought I could ever be to a woman, but I want to get to know you even better, and I think it's important to be open in a relationship." Ricardo paused, as if he was expecting a reaction from her. She wasn't going to give him that satisfaction. He may have stolen her heart, but he hadn't crushed all dignity.

He took a deep breath. "I know why you're upset with me, and if things go the way I hope they will, then you'll find out everything. The whole truth, but it's going to take two of us to make this work. I need answers too. I'd like to know where all the money went. I'm confused by it because you seem so frugal. The only decent clothes and jewellery you have are what I've given you. You never go shopping or partying on your own. So, will you put me out of my misery? What happened to it all?"

Helen was speechless as she watched him thoughtfully munch on some marinated anchovies. He must be blissfully lacking any sense of morality or fair play in the way he conducted his businesses. And he'd been pretty deadpan discussing his abandoned son, so she doubted anything she said would shock him. Why the hell not tell him? She had nothing to lose. He was turning out to be a hard-faced, devious bastard, so she'd give him as good as he was giving everyone else. Perhaps all he really did need was sex and speedboats.

Her tone was deliberately belligerent. "Okay, you want to know? Million number one went on, let's just say, *bills*. Million number two is invested for the future. For my financial security, to realize my plans and dreams."

"You have dreams?"

"And aspirations, yes." She ground her teeth together for a second before continuing. "I want to make a difference somehow – even if it's just in a small way."

Ricardo made a beckoning movement with his hand. "Please carry on."

She felt like slapping him but continued. "I've been thinking about setting up an independent outlet for all the local farmers and producers back home. A chain of farm shops maybe, regular farmers' markets and a hamper service stocked with local produce that we could market on the Internet. Some foraging courses too, maybe." She took a swig of juice. "Nothing firm yet, but the idea is to give everyone the chance of a decent living, over which they have total control."

"It sounds very noble."

"I want to help everyone fight off all the bloody builders and supermarkets who don't give the local community a second thought. We're all sick of ruthless developers. If something isn't done soon, there'll be no estuary or marshland left because it'll be full of hooting yachties that come down in the summer, trash the place, and then disappear. It's become quite obvious that the only chance we have is to band together and fight for our way of life."

"Very admirable," Ricardo said with a skeptical turn of his head. "But you'll have a hard job beating off determined developers, because money is power. And let's not forget that building marinas, apartments, and other infrastructure creates a lot of work."

"So you think it's justified?"

"I don't see anything wrong in creating jobs for people who couldn't otherwise live in such a beautiful area. Jobs for people who can't work the land or produce artisan treats for rich people with spare cash. Your exclusive little backwater isn't that different from somewhere like Malaga. Everyone would like to live there undisturbed on a wee little estate with rolling hills and jam for tea. But they can't, it's as simple as that. And you don't want them to either, do you?"

"How dare you say that? You have no idea what I want."

He shot her a chilling look and continued unabashed. "Have you done the 'people sums' with this magnificently philanthropic idea? How many farmers' cozy livelihoods would be assured versus a headcount of new people being able to move into the area and enjoy it? Your dream seems a tiny bit selfish and insular, if you ask me. Perhaps you need to rethink it."

Helen flushed with outrage. "You don't know what you're talking about. Once the place has been concreted over no one but the superrich will be able to afford to live there. Me included."

"I don't accept that," Ricardo said sternly. "Whatever happens, there will be rich and poor in every community. You're always going to need people for the roads and bins, the schools, shops, the day-to-day grind of it all. There's always a place for the people who have to live off tinned food on a daily basis, not your lovely organic, free-range samphire. So why do their children have to choke away in the slums of the inner city? Can't they have a chance to live by the sea too?" His nostrils flared. "You don't realize how lucky you were to grow up where you did, Helen, and you're not exactly poor now."

"Well, listen to you, Ricardo Almanza! I shouldn't think you've ever emptied a dustbin in your life!"

He shrugged. "I don't live in an ivory tower."

"Maybe it is a case of 'not in my backyard,'" Helen said. "But how would you feel if someone plonked a noisy caravan site right next to your estate and then you found rubbish washing up on your spotless beach?

"Couldn't happen. I own everything around here, even the beach."

"Yes, I know. But what if you didn't have the money to defend it? What if you had no choice, like your dad when he lost the department store?"

"I fixed that, remember? And I'll fix anything that gets in my way or threatens me and the people I care about."

"Presumably that includes Pirro. Well, bravo, Ricardo. Bravo for protecting yourself with your billions. It's pretty easy not to take no for an answer when you're loaded, surrounded by sycophants, and you want something badly enough, isn't it? Just like a spoiled child!"

"*Dios!* You're prickly this afternoon, Helen! I know you're pissed off about Antonella, but so am I! Or is it because you didn't eat much at lunch?" He offered her some olives, but she shook her head. "Lucia's not going for another couple of hours. Shall I get her to fix you something?"

"Do what you like. That's what you normally do, isn't it?"

Including trying to steal my parents' farm by marrying me...

"I think maybe this conversation has run its course for now." Ricardo shook his head and frowned. "Listen, I need to touch base with the office and make sure Antonella clears off. There's a shareholder who needs some urgent attention and is causing some disruption. So while I deal with those irritations, I'll send Lucia up with a proper drink and a snack for you. With any luck, it should improve your mood and we can have a reasonable conversation later."

Helen froze. Ricardo bent to place a kiss on the top of her head. "*Me vuelves loco*, you drive me crazy," he whispered in a heavy voice before leaving her. He did it every time, pressed a secret button inside of her that maintained his control on her. How could she still be so lethally drawn to him? How much damage was she going to allow him to do to her already battered heart?

A few minutes later, Lucia arrived with an iced bottle of expensive imported Prosecco and a tray of tapas.

"Senor, he say it's your favorite," she said shyly and hovered for a moment.

Helen's voice sounded weak. "Thank you, Lucia. Senor Almanza is very good at remembering such details."

Lucia shuffled a few inches and then turned to leave, but seemed to change her mind as she wrung her hands slightly. "The lady, the Condesa's new woman," she said and fretted her bottom lip. "She say she must speak to Senor Ricardo, very rude. She insult me so." She closed her eyes and crossed herself quickly. "Please forgive me, Senora. I hit her with a wooden spoon and say…*vete al cuerno*!"

"Oh Lucia!" Helen laughed with surprise. Lady Lidia being told to piss off by one of the staff was priceless. "She's no friend of mine, believe me. You did the right thing, and if she ever turns up again—"

"I send her packing. *Bueno*!"

The old woman shuffled off happily and Helen's moment of delight quickly faded. Lidia Skiptree was a viper, cunning in wheedling her way into the Condesa's employ, and it looked like she was trying to stir up trouble with Ricardo from what Lucia had said too. Or perhaps she wanted reconciliation with her old lover while she was here.

Helen recalled the Condesa's advice on the day she'd left her job in Ibiza—the Almanza men destroyed their lovers in the end. She had been warned. It was unlikely that Lidia was the only woman scorned at losing such a prize catch as Ricardo Almanza, and she was unlikely to be the last. And all this was heading for a very sad and sorry end as far as Helen was concerned too. Ricardo had no deeper feelings for her than any other convenient bed partner. It just so happened he'd married her for convenience.

Helen poured herself some Prosecco and took a deep gulp from her glass. They'd only been married for a couple of weeks and he was back to work already taking that phone call, but she had no right to begrudge him that. This had only ever been a business transaction. It wasn't Ricardo's fault she'd gone and fallen in love with him, wanted more than he had contracted. But she wasn't going to let him drive her parents out of their home after all this. Ideally, she'd get on a plane back to the UK as quickly as possible and try to forget this period of her life. But she'd signed a contract. She was legally obliged to play her part for three months however difficult it was going to be. If there was some way she could walk out now she would, but she had to check the legalities first. She had to protect her family.

Chapter Fourteen

Ricardo suddenly realized he was muttering to himself as he stalked up to his office. It was a massive annoyance having his honeymoon interrupted by some idiot who couldn't cope with a persistent small-time shareholder. What he could do from there was anyone's guess, but if it got the stupid cow out of his staff's hair until he got back, he'd do it. It would also give Helen some breathing space. Perhaps he had been smothering her. She hadn't had any time to herself since they'd married, and she probably wasn't used to it, being an only child and living on her own all this time.

He punched in the phone number he'd been given by headquarters. Skiptree Enterprises...Finance Director... it rang a bell, but he couldn't place it. His business interests were vast, complicated, and diverse.

"Hello, Ricky," the husky female voice purred down the line. "Just thought I'd ring to pass on my congrats. Saw a few of your wedding snaps in *Rizzo Magazine*. Nice. You look good as always, but I'm amazed at your choice of bride." She sounded breathless. "Thought you'd tired of pale, English girls. Brazilian seemed to be more your style the last time I noticed."

"This is an unpleasant surprise, Kat, and characteristically vulgar, but then you always were trailer trash underneath all the bling. I'm just glad I never actually shagged you. I thought I told you not to bother me anymore. I blocked your number months ago."

"I changed it. You can hang up now, because I'm right behind you."

"What?" Ricardo span around to see Lidia lounging against the marble archway that led into the inner part of his study. She waved her cell phone at him with one hand as her other clutched a bottle of cooking brandy. "What the hell are you doing here? How did you find me? For Christ's sake, you've been warned about doing this—"

"I want to speak to you, darling, that's all. Don't be nasty. I'm only hazarding a guess, but I assume Saint Helen managed to convince you she was a virgin, that you claimed the ultimate prize when you married her?" She cackled unpleasantly. "I expect she said she'd been hanging on for years, you know, waiting for Mr. Right to come along. Well, it's rubbish. My brother, Roger, had her when she was fifteen, broke her in for all the low rent aristos that followed. Not to mention a gang of construction workers once. Her antics in the barn were legendary. Still, it made her enough money to go to university and travel. Scheming little madam."

Ricardo ground his teeth with anger and revulsion. "What exactly do you think you're going to achieve by breaking in here and slandering my wife? You've never even met her. Have you no dignity? I'll say this once and for all—I am not interested in you."

She placed the bottle of brandy onto a nearby wooden dresser with deliberate precision. "Oh but I *have* met her, darling. We went to the same school. Talk about a small world.

Who'd have thought you'd end up marrying the local druggy tart? Of course, I'm *sure* she's cleaned up her act these days, but could you credit it? Marshall never got caught shifting the stuff in that barn, but that was where plenty of unsuspecting college kids got hooked. And then she sent the big boys in when they couldn't pay up. "

"You're mad, psychotic."

"It must be an Almanza thing, drawn to the same sort of colorful women," she said excitedly. "Brave old you, Ricardo, you finally managed to tame her, but don't get yourself into a total pickle like Primeiro, will you, darling? We all saw the headlines at head office when *that* happened. Such a tragedy. She may seem sweet, but she's not. I'd hate to see history repeating itself. One family destroyed is enough, you have no idea what she's capable of."

"I've heard enough of your disgusting lies."

"You don't believe me, do you?" She threw her phone down onto a sofa and began to unbutton her blouse.

"Of course I don't believe you, you're just being malicious. A stalker gone mad with jealously."

"Then I suggest you ask your beautiful new bride all about it." She peeled off her top to reveal a scarlet lace bra, and dropped it on the floor. "Ask her about Roger Humby in the barn and then watch your little bride blush."

"I can destroy you, Kat."

She pouted. "Don't call me Kat anymore. I hate that common name."

Ricardo clenched his fists as she slipped the bra straps down over her shoulders. "I can think of a few names that would suit you right now."

She began to slide down the zip of her skirt. "Call me baby," she breathed and licked her lips. "Or your bitch…"

"Stop this ridiculous charade immediately!"

"You don't mean that, Ricky. I know you don't," she said and stepped out of her skirt as she drew closer. "I wore my best underwear for you, darling. She'd never do that for you, not in a million years, but I will. I'll do *anything*."

Ricardo gave her shoulder a firm shove with the flat of his hand as she reached out to touch him. "Then put your clothes back on, get out, and stay away from us or you'll regret it."

She glared at him and there was a silent impasse until she sulkily picked up her skirt. "We'll just have to see about that, won't we? Well, good luck with Miss Snooty Drawers and when it's all over, you *now* have my number. Tell that Rottweiler secretary of yours to put me through next time."

He nodded towards the brandy bottle. "How much of that have you had?"

"Nothing yet. I pinched it from your miserable cook when she wasn't looking. Thought we could enjoy it together. In bed."

"You thought wrong. You're fit to drive, so…" He thrust her blouse at her. "Drive away fast before I call the police."

"But the Condesa—"

"I'll deal with her."

"You know where I am," she said defiantly over her shoulder as she went to leave. "And I'll do anything, remember. *Anything…*"

Once out of sight, Ricardo slammed down the silent phone he'd been clutching throughout the clumsy striptease, his head ready to burst with anger and confusion. Could there be any truth in what she had said? Was it possible that Helen had been involved with drugs? The woman he had fallen in love had been a supplier? Like the scum that had lived off his brother's wife before it destroyed her?

He angrily threw the phone onto the polished table and it slithered with a crash to the floor. If that were true, Helen was probably responsible for destroying others' lives and families. If it hadn't been for dealer trash like that he would still have a brother and a mother, maybe even his dad would still be alive. And Pirro…poor innocent little baby Pirro would have grown up with his real parents.

This couldn't be happening! Just ten minutes earlier he'd had been on the verge of asking Helen Marshall to remain his wife, because he had fallen in love with her. But how could that happen now, with so many questions that needed to be answered? How could he explain to Pirro that he had married such a woman, a woman who peddled death, one of the parasites of the world were responsible his parents' deaths? Ricardo's love for her could never be enough to get him through that sort of emotional storm.

His blood ran cold as his mind began to race faster. If there was any truth to this, who was to say Helen was off the drugs? They'd met in Ibiza, the White Isle, where sex, drugs, and parties were the norm. She'd been his captive for a couple of weeks and, now he thought about it, she *was* behaving strangely. Irritable, irrational, especially about that stupid old handbag. The handbag she took with her everywhere…she was agitated they'd left it behind at their picnic. What could it contain that was so important to her that he couldn't easily replace? Or wouldn't replace. His heart turned to stone. Could her behavior be withdrawal symptoms? It would explain everything, including the money. One million euros on 'bills.' Some bills…

Ricardo slammed his hands painfully onto his desk in a desperate attempt to feel something, anything but the sickening lurch in his stomach.

How could he have screwed up so badly? Maybe it *was* genetic, this male Almanza self-destructive tendency, their weakness for evil women. His smart big brother hadn't spotted it, neither had Dad, so why the hell did Ricardo think he was immune? Arrogance, that was why. Arrogance and stupidity. He had always lambasted gullible people, but look at the bloody state of him now. On his knees, emotionally. He was a disaster.

"I'm not accepting this," he muttered to the empty room and was disturbed by the emotion in his own voice. "I'm not going to let this happen." He had to clear this up, give her a chance to prove that it was all a pack of lies. It had to be lies.

• • •

Ricardo reached the terrace and silently watched Helen pour herself another glass of wine. The bottle was half-empty already.

"You made it back then," Helen said when he appeared next to her. "I suspected you'd be gone all afternoon attending to 'business'."

"Obviously," Ricardo said with a frown and glanced at the bottle. "But we need to talk."

"Oh not about the rights and wrongs of property development again, *please*," Helen said, and took a large drink from her glass.

"No." He put his elbows firmly onto the table. "I want to talk about Roger Humby."

Helen's head jerked backwards in surprise and then she couldn't stop an incredulous laugh escaping. "Oh, I can guess who you've been talking to! Popped in to see you too, did she? It really is a small world when it comes to backhanded property development, isn't it?" She didn't think she could stomach his deceit much longer, not when he was looking at her with the beautiful hazel eyes that never failed to melt her resolve. Until now, the bastard. He'd obviously been cooking up his next move with Lidia, Kat, whatever persona she'd been using to get to him. Right under her nose practically, the pair of them. What nerve! Perhaps they'd planned today's horrible visit together from the very start. What next? Blackmail?

"You don't deny knowing her?"

"Of course not, why should I? We were in the same year at school."

"Best friends, I heard."

"Hardly that," Helen said. "She was queen of all the bullies. Still is. And I guess it's now safe for me to believe her when she says that you two have also met?"

Ricardo nodded. "It's a small world."

"Isn't it? I'm surprised you haven't invited her to join us here for cocktails. Or dinner maybe, that would really make my day."

"She left some time ago," he said and then his voice grew quiet. "You partied, you two? In your parents' barn?"

"Only in a small way and it happened in everybody's barn," Helen said and pushed her sunglasses back on her head. She didn't care if he noticed her eyes were dull and red. "I don't know what she's been telling you, but it's bound to be an exaggeration. She was never invited to our little parties, even her brother couldn't stand her in those days."

Ricardo took a deep breath and knotted his fingers together tightly. "She alluded to a level of substance abuse, your supply…"

Helen sat stunned for a moment and absentmindedly took another swig of Prosecco. Why on earth had the little witch dragged up the illicit bottle of cider incident? It had been naughty, pinching it from the cupboard, but she'd only had one sip before Kat swanned off with it into the woods with a French exchange student.

"Hardly a big deal, Ricardo!" Helen shrugged at the

pettiness of it all. "Everyone does it at some time or another, don't they? Part of growing up, but if we're getting puritanical here, I admit it was probably a silly thing to do. If I'd been caught Dad would have hit the roof, but I don't really regret it. Schoolgirl hijinks, that's all.

Ricardo glared angrily at her. "What if someone got out of their depth?"

He really was sanctimonious when he wanted to be. "I hardly think anyone needed me to introduce them to the delights of underage indulgence. I was by far the youngest and least experienced of our crowd." She looked at him crossly. "So where's all this leading? That all happened a long time ago, kids being kids. I do hope you're not going to make an issue out of it."

"You seem almost proud of what you did."

She was tempted to giggle at the craziness of the situation, and the wine was doing its worst on her empty stomach. "Oh come on! Millions of teenagers do the same sort of thing every single day, and don't go off the rails, they do it for a while, get sick and then grow up." She suddenly remembered what he'd told her about his sister-in-law, which would explain why his expression was so bleak, his eyes so angry. "Look, I don't want to sound flippant, but not everyone ends up going down the drain like Arabella. Some people are destined to push things too far. For all you know her finger had been on the self-destruct button for years."

"You seem particularly unmoved by the appalling tragedy of it all," Ricardo replied bitterly.

"I'm sorry if it seems that way, but I didn't know her. I didn't know your brother and mother either. In fact, I'm not sure I know you as well as I thought I did."

Ricardo's expression was unreadable. "Can I assume you still enjoy such social stimulants?"

Helen regarded her half-empty glass, irritated by his absurdly highhanded tone. He was treating her like a child, like someone helpless he could control. "Yes, I bloody do. I'm an adult, aren't I?" She rebelliously topped it up and slammed the bottle back into the ice bucket. Ricardo was turning out to be more of a control freak than she had expected. He'd sent Lucia up with the wine, hadn't he? Was he expecting her to ask permission?

"You've had too much to drink, Helen. I don't like it."

"Grounds for divorce, is it?"

"I think maybe it will do, yes," Ricardo said coldly.

Helen's breath caught for a second. "What are you saying?"

"What I am saying, Helen, is that I might as well bring the divorce forward if you insist on behaving like this. There's no reason why we have to drag this unpleasant sham out for three months if you're not happy after all." He pushed his chair abruptly away from the table and Helen's wine glass wobbled. "I'll get on to the lawyers as soon as possible and have an addendum drawn up."

Helen's head was spinning. "Just like that?"

"Just like that." He sniffed and stood up, overshadowing her with an air of menace. "Unless you have anything you wish to add."

Helen began to panic slightly. He'd turned the tables on her so quickly she hadn't been able to deal with the other poisonous seed that The Bully had planted.

"I need some assurance regarding what's mine and yours. I should have read the small print, I know."

"Anything you can put on your body is yours. Everything else we brought into this marriage reverts to its original owner. That *is* the point of a pre-nup after all." He let out a hollow laugh. "Christ! You don't want some more money already, do you?"

"No, Ricardo, I just need to be sure you have no claim on anything in the UK," she said stiffly.

"Don't be ridiculous! Why on earth would I want anything of yours? I don't want anything you have to offer, Helen. I don't even want to look at you anymore."

His words hurt, but anger gave her courage. "You do bore quickly."

Ricardo looked down on her with a disgusted expression on his face. "You might as well finish that," he said, pointing at the Prosecco." It's the last thing you're ever going to get out of me."

He stiffly turned and walked away back towards the villa, his tall angular frame silhouetted for a few seconds against the pale blue sunset. She watched him go with a twisted sense of longing and anger. She wanted to run after him and say she forgave him for treating her so abysmally, that she'd do anything, be anything he wanted, if she could only stay with him for a little longer.

But she had known this was going to happen in the end. It had been inevitable and Ricardo had made no secret of the fact from the very beginning. If only she hadn't allowed herself that small grain of hope that there could be some sort of a happy ending.

A chill was settling like mist over the hard stones and metal of the terrace and Helen swallowed back the tears when she heard the sound of an engine being started and then tires spinning on gravel.

She would probably never see him again.

Chapter Fifteen

The clouds were beginning to gather everywhere when Helen arrived back at Primrose Farm. Although she'd cleared the legal bills and given her parents a fighting fund to finish the initial court case, the aggravation was still rumbling slowly on. It had never really gone away. Something new seemed to be around every corner to cause anxiety.

It had been three weeks since Helen had returned from Spain and the Skiptree estate was blatantly running their animals over the Marshall's land, causing damage and upsetting their livestock. And then there were the "travelers" that seemed to be spookily well-heeled with their Range Rovers and designer clothes, intimidating the local families and setting fires all over the place. They were clever, of course. The police appeared to have their hands tied and the legal system was way too slow and cumbersome to tackle the ever-changing nature of the harassment.

All the landowners knew was that if the trespassers were allowed to continue in this way, eventually commoner's rights would prevail and the land would be lost to them forever. But the costs of fighting their corner were crippling. It was unfair and it was bullying, but it was like trying to hold back the rising tide. However long they battled, they would never win, not up against the cold-blooded millions that were behind it all. It was just a question of who fell first. And then the Skiptree Estate and Fothergill Enterprises would have their marina.

Helen hated to admit it, but maybe it was getting to the stage where they should consider their position and quit while they could. It would never be that simple though. Her father was approaching retirement age officially, although he'd always said he'd die on the job. It had been his entire life, he loved it, and he wanted to spend his last days here on Primrose Farm.

Her mother's voice interrupted her thoughts as she stood in the farm kitchen. "So when are you planning on telling us, Helen?"

"What do you mean, Mum?" Helen rubbed a cloth round a cracked mug and pretended to inspect it closely.

Mrs. Marshall beat some cake batter more vigorously. "It's not like you to avoid eye contact with me, dear."

Helen frowned and rubbed the mug harder. "Don't be daft. I don't know what you're talking about."

"Then look me straight in the face and tell me you're *not* pregnant then, will you?"

"What?" She hadn't seen that question coming, and it heralded a sweep of pent up emotion she hadn't realized was there. Suddenly the previous few weeks seemed to crash down upon her and Helen was horrified to feel a tear tip over her bottom lashes and trickle down her cheek. She put the mug down on the drainer with a clunk and rubbed at her eye with the heel of her hand.

"Oh come here." Mrs. Marshall gathered her only child into her arms and tucked her damp face against her chest. "It'll be all right, love. You didn't think we'd be angry, did you?"

Helen tasted the cold salt drip that rolled into her mouth and her throat ached. "I don't know what to think. I've made such a mess of everything."

"Everything will be fine, we'll manage somehow, assuming that you...?"

Helen stared up and felt completely empty. "I'm not pregnant, Mum."

Her mother looked anxious and stroked Helen's hair. "Are you sure? You seem different. I can sense a change in you."

"I'm sure."

"Are you? Completely?" The older woman's tone became suspiciously cheerful as she squeezed Helen's shoulder before saying, "I've always dreamt of there being a new baby on Primrose Farm."

"I put on quite a bit of weight in Spain, that's all. Too much high living. It'll come off soon enough."

Helen's spine stiffened as her mother's gaze slipped to her stomach area and she frowned. "I don't want to pry, sweetheart, but you both seemed so happy..."

Helen sighed, her shoulders felt very heavy. "It's so complicated. I love him, Mum, in spite of everything. I know it's ridiculous, but I can't help it and you going on about wanting a baby around isn't making me feel any better about it all."

"You'd tell Ricardo if you were though, wouldn't you?" her mother asked gently. "He'd have a right to know."

"He wouldn't be interested, believe me, Mum. It's not his first if you get my meaning."

"Really?" Mrs. Marshall winced awkwardly. "Oh I see... well at least you two were *married*."

They still were legally.

"And I wouldn't trap him like that even if I was pregnant," Helen said quickly. "If we had an accident he'd just think I was after his money."

"Perhaps you should make an appointment at the clinic just to be on the safe side, to make sure—"

"I'm not pregnant, okay?" At least she was as sure as she could be that she wasn't. All the signs were that she was about to have the period from hell any minute now. Sore breasts, bloating, headache, tearfulness… And it was better that way, she told herself firmly. Ricardo was finished with her and already had an inconvenient heir. It was over. *This is the last thing you're getting from me* were his last words to her and she was sure he'd meant it. "It's bad enough having a failed marriage behind me so soon anyway, let alone an unplanned pregnancy." She wiped her eyes with the tissue her mum gave her. "Dad would hit the roof."

"I wouldn't be so sure about that."

"He'd be pretty angry."

"He's sad that you've split up with Ricardo, but he'd never be cross about a baby."

Helen's father may have taken the news quietly, but Helen knew he was disappointed. He had always been one to keep his feelings to himself on delicate matters and Helen couldn't work out if it was her or Ricardo he was most angry with. The phone began to ring at the other end of the house and once her mother had gone to answer it, her mind began to wander. Her parents had never said as much, but Helen knew they had yearned for sons, to help out with the farm, to continue the work of generations. Helen knew she couldn't cope with running a large farm on her own. Thank goodness she wasn't pregnant.

• • •

"I'm afraid I have bad news," Mr. Marshall announced three hours later as the lunchtime dishes were being cleared away. "Bob Hargreaves popped over during morning milking to tell me. He's selling up Pinkmead and the other two farms adjoining us are about to sign it all away too." He puffed out his cheeks and rubbed his eyes under his spectacles. "So, girls…it's just us left." He stood abruptly and Helen's heart turned over painfully as she saw his bottom lip twitch. "I'll be off to the calves now."

Helen exchanged a glance with her mother. He left the house and they watched as his old rounded shoulders seemed to shrink a little more as he trudged up the yard in the lashing rain. The strain of the troubled farm was beginning to show again.

"Katie needs some TLC in the barn, if you could," Mrs. Marshall said in her most stiff upper-lipped way. "All those new kittens are wearing her out. Would you mind popping up to check on her?"

"Will do," Helen said softly, knowing that her mum needed a private, dignified moment alone. She wondered if she might cry. She'd never seen her mum weep, but things had never seemed quite as hopeless as this before.

The barn was warm and dry at least when she reached it, a safe haven from the elements and the sweet smelling hay bales muffled the clatter of rain on the corrugated iron roof. Helen crouched to pick up a tiny squirming ball of fur and its high-pitched mew made her feel even more tearful. She set the tiny, warm and defenceless kitten back down into its cardboard box nest. It had been lined with an old red blanket and Katie the cat closed her yellow eyes for a moment as Helen stroked her head. "Thank you for letting me hold him," she whispered. "He's perfect." Her hand dropped to her stomach. She felt an all too familiar ache, then she heard something fall with a soft thump to the floor.

"Hello, Helen." The voice behind her was unmistakeable. Ricardo.

Helen scrambled to her feet, her heart pounding louder and faster than the rain on the barn's roof. She spun round and stared at him, cold with shock. "What's happened to you?"

He was unshaven, hair matted to his head, raindrops trickling over his sharp cheekbones, glistening against the stubble on his jaw. Dressed in a black leather jacket and black jeans, his white T-shirt was splattered with mud and his breath formed short bursts of mist in the damp air.

"It's disgusting out there, if you hadn't noticed. Your bloody farmyard is covered in crap and I've been running."

"Running?" Helen said, suddenly seeing the funny side of a *dirty* Ricardo Almanza, but feeling instinctively wary. He had no good reason for being there. "I didn't think you'd know how. Don't you have *people* for that sort of indignity?"

"Funny," he growled, brushing away some barley straw that had latched on to the soaked denim of his jeans.

Helen's heart sank when his volcanic expression registered and any levity of the situation evaporated. His eyes flashed in a way she'd not seen since their wedding day, when he'd lashed Jerardo Capella away from her. This was one angry hulk of Spanish male. But, of course, how stupid of her. He was there because of the marina, because of Primrose Farm, nothing to do with his runaway sham wife. This was the last piece of his corporate puzzle, his bankers bonus. He'd come to end it once and for all.

Well, she could do angry as well and was now growing too furious and protective to be intimidated by him. It was just the two of them there and if she had to fight like an alley cat to save what she had left then she would. She'd beaten him up once before, after all.

"We have unfinished business," Ricardo said coldly.

"Come to wield the fatal blow, have you? I guess you've brought the marriage contract addendum for me to sign? And now we're the only farm left fighting you've come to finish that off too. In person." Helen clamped her teeth together to stop herself shaking before she continued. "Well, let me tell you this, Almanza, we're not going without a fight and if it has to be dirty one, then bring it on."

"I've come for my wife and child."

Helen felt her limbs turn to stone as he ran a shaking hand through the ink black shock of hair plastered to his forehead. His wedding ring glinted in the grey light that filtered through a dusty cobwebbed window.

"You've what?"

"I waited as long as I could before coming. I've been holed up in London since you got back here, like a cat on a hot tin roof waiting for the phone to ring."

"In London?"

"I had to be somewhere close, so that I could get here within a couple of hours when the time was right. Your mother said you needed time to get your head together, to decide what you really wanted without being influenced, so I should stay away. But what she said today was just too much."

"My mother? You've been talking to each other behind my back?"

"We spoke on the phone soon after you got back and she gave me the tongue lashing of a life time. *Dios*! I thought Lucia was bad! Berated me for abandoning my responsibilities, called me things that would make a pimp blush —"

"So, let me get this straight. My mum told you I was pregnant?" Helen shook her head in disbelief. "Talk about interfering..."

"She couldn't stop herself from telling me when I rang

this morning, and it was the last straw. Why I couldn't wait any longer. Your mother didn't betray you. She wants what's best for you, that's all. She was protecting you."

Helen's brain was racing. "Look there's been a misunderstanding. You really didn't need to come."

"Didn't need to come? This is our child we're talking about! Why would I want to miss a second of my baby?"

"Because you've done it all before?" Her voice sounded brittle. She *felt* brittle.

"What?"

"Pirro?" Helen said bitterly. "Remember him? Your son and heir?"

"Pirro isn't mine!"

"Oh I see, so whose is he then? Jerardo Capella sneaked in and gave your girlfriend one while you were out on business, did he? Or don't you really care who his real father is, just as long as you're not landed with the inconvenience, the responsibility!"

Ricardo took a step towards her, his hands tense, jaw set. Helen could see the veins on his hands.

"Pirro is…" Ricardo shook his head from side to side, as if he was attempting to control his temper. "Pirro is my brother's son, my nephew. I love him, obviously, but he is not my son! If I'd thought for one minute you'd thought that—"

Helen was in such a state of shock that she couldn't think *anything* for a few moments and couldn't find her voice before he continued.

"Listen, I have no doubt I'm the father of this child." He paused and exhaled silently as she shook her head. "So we need to deal with all this sensibly."

Helen slumped down onto a bale of hay, her legs weak and shaky. *Sensible, yes, she needed to be sensible. Sensible was good.*

"I can help you clean up, Helen, before it's too late. We can make a go of this, fix everything."

"Clean up?" Helen frowned with annoyance. "Are you trying to be funny? I live on a farm for goodness sake. Besides, look at you!"

"Don't be difficult, you know what I'm talking about. I've already booked a suite in one of the best Swiss clinics. It will work out just fine, I know it."

"Ricardo, have you gone quite mad?"

"The drugs, Helen, all the stuff that used to go on in here." He gestured around them with both arms, his movements jerky. It wasn't like him. She'd never seen him on the verge of losing control. "You'll have the best specialists, nobody need ever know."

"This is ridiculous. The only drug I've ever used is Acetaminophen…" She leant back against a wall of rough straw and raised her eyes to the spidery rafters, she suddenly felt very tired. "I've never moved in your sort of circles, Ricardo. It's not my world. The first champagne I ever tasted was with you. Why on earth do you think I'm a user?"

"Kat Humby told me you were."

"I should have guessed. So you took her word for it? Thanks a lot! You really are a stupid—"

"I tried talking to you about it, that last night in Menorca. You didn't deny it so what was I supposed to think? And you were behaving irrationally, you said some hurtful things."

"You hurt me too…and I'd drunk too much on an empty stomach."

"I didn't want to believe what she'd told me, found it hard to, but the facts were being thrown in my face and it all started to make sense."

"It did? Care to share these 'facts'? This I have got to hear!"

"Very well. First there's the money. Drugs would be a reason why you needed so much, so quickly and why you wouldn't elaborate on what your 'bills' were."

"It's still none of your business, but I'm telling you now it wasn't drug money!"

"I know where it went now, Helen. Your mum told me everything, about how you paid off all their debts." His expression was pained. "You could have told me, I wouldn't have judged."

"Oh Mother!" Helen was totally exasperated with the pair of them now. "So much for discretion! Dad's such a proud, private man, I don't think he could stand it if—"

"He knows that I know."

"Did you tell them how I got all that money as well?" Unable to look him in the face she saw him nod from the corner of her eye. "Oh God, they'll be so ashamed."

Ricardo touched her lightly on the elbow, just enough to reassure her and then let his hand drop. "They're humbled, proud that you'd marry someone you didn't love just to help them. They love you in spite of and because of that. But getting back to the 'facts', our last evening together—"

"Do we have to?" She was beginning to feel shivery.

"Yes, we do. You were behaving as if you were coming down off a high, as if you needed a fix but couldn't get one, which made sense because you were out of touch with your dodgy Ibiza friends, your supply."

"Oh, not Bjorn again! You're obsessed with the poor man. Being gay wasn't enough to get the poor guy off the hook. You had to make him my imaginary dealer! Bjorn's body is a temple to all things organic and vegetarian, darling, he doesn't even smoke!"

"I admit I don't like him, he makes me feel…jealous."

Helen couldn't help letting out a small laugh. "Mad dog

Almanza."

"And then you got really agitated about losing your handbag." He gestured behind him to a brown heap in the corner. "I suddenly realized that you took it everywhere with you, even to the fire at Tino's, and when I offered to replace it and its contents you didn't want to. Why is that, Helen? What do you keep in there that's so crucial? What's in there that my money can't, or *won't*, buy if it's not illegal drugs?"

Helen stood up and stared at the handbag on the floor. She'd heard it drop to the floor before she'd realized he was there. "You found it."

"I went looking for it after we argued. I had to take Antonella back to Mahon. The last thing I wanted was for her to make matters even worse by her hanging around, and then I searched until it got dark. I used the torch I keep in the car until I found it. By the time I returned you were gone. I waited for you, stayed awake all night, but you never came back."

"You'd said it was over between us. I assumed I wasn't going to see you again anyway." She shrugged, still staring at the bag. "What was the point in me hanging on? I caught the next flight home."

"I had to phone your parents in the end just to make sure you were safe, and not in a ditch somewhere. They wanted to know what had happened, of course, so I told them."

Helen solemnly looked at the feet. "So what did you think once you'd gone through my handbag?"

"I've never opened it."

"Then there's no time like the present." She marched over to the bundle of brown leather and thrust it under his nose. "Go on, open it!"

"No, it makes no difference to how I feel about you."

"Then I'll do it!" She ripped open the zip and tipped the entire contents on the ground. Lipstick, sunglasses and mints fell with a clatter, tampons rolled, tissues and assorted bits of paper floated after them. "There you go! Satisfied now?"

Ricardo stooped to pick up two L-shaped plastic containers, one brown, one blue. "I had no idea."

"I didn't want you to know."

"But why not? You should have told me in case—"

"My asthma's perfectly well controlled as long as I take the brown inhaler twice a day and have the blue one with me at all times in case I have an attack. The pollen on the hill was bad that day, and the pines were in flower and Lucia's cat had been on our bed again."

"And those things set it off?"

"I'm allergic to them, so yes, but I was also very angry and emotional. I was going to need the blue one soon, I could just tell. That's why I was so anxious and irritable. And wheezy. Bloody marvelous state of affairs for a farmer's daughter, isn't it?"

"For God's sake, why the big secret? There must be millions of asthmatics in the world."

"I hate being labeled, really hate it. I don't want people to think I want their sympathy, I don't. I'm fine most of the time, so nobody needs to know, nobody has a reason to bully me either."

"Let me guess, Kat Humby bullied you because of this?"

"And her gang of posh friends. They had a lovely time, because I wore National Health free glasses until I was sixteen too. And braces on my teeth."

"You'd never guess to look at you now."

"Nope, my teeth are straight and I saved up for eye surgery to fix them. Unfortunately, all the money in the world can't buy me better lungs."

He pushed a hand deep into the inside pocket of his jacket. "I'm so sorry."

"Don't be. I'm fine."

"I'm sorry for accusing you of using drugs. It was stupid of me to come to such a wild conclusion based on, based on nothing more than me being irrational. And believing a mad woman's poisonous lies."

Helen straightened her shoulders. She had the upper hand now. "So you might be able to get this farm from us with all your millions and your gang of lawyers, but you're not going to paint me as an addict to take the baby you think I'm carrying."

Ricardo's eyes opened wide and his mouth fell open. "You think I'm capable of that?"

"Yes, Ricardo. Yes I do and why shouldn't I after everything you've done so far? You and your sneaky subsidiaries have cut quite a swathe through the landscape here. We both know Primrose Farm is the last property left on the peninsula that you've not gotten your hands on and that we can't fight you much longer." She threw her arms in the air with desperation. "I wish you'd deny it all, Ricardo. I wish you could say that all this buying of land isn't down to Lidia Skiptree and you."

"I've only ever known her as *Humby*, Kat Humby. I didn't realize she'd changed her name and that she'd bought a stake in Fothergill Enterprises." His expression darkened. "So, I had no idea my company was involved with hers, either, until I started investigating this marina project while I was in London this week."

Helen didn't try to hide the sarcasm in her voice. "Really?"

"Really! She pulled the wool over a lot of people's eyes trying to get close to me again, but she's out of a job now and the police will be knocking on her door very soon. So not only is she a bully, Helen, she's also a stalker."

"Bloody hell…"

"It's true. She tried to seduce me into having sex with her

at a property conference in London a few years back. It wasn't hard turning her down, believe me, there are limits even when it is being handed to you on a plate. But she couldn't let it go."

"So you and her never…"

"No! Only in her warped fantasies, and then when she saw our wedding pictures it must have sent her right over the top. She lost it completely." He took a deep breath before continuing. "But, even though she's out of the picture now, I have to tell you that the recent property acquisitions you mentioned *are* all down to me personally."

"I knew it." Helen slumped down onto the bale of hay with the cat box on it and put her head in her hands.

"I've bought all fifty square miles of the estuary land, except Primrose Farm."

She felt sick. "And you plan on getting it any way you can presumably?"

"No."

"Yeah, right."

"I don't want your farm, I never have, and I'll do everything to make sure that it will be here forever, for all future Marshall generations."

"You're confusing me now. Is this some sort of warped bargain? Stay out of my life, keep your mouth shut, and I won't take your home away from you?"

He suddenly had a look of total desperation about him. "Please believe me. I had no idea about the extent of the marina development because it was a subsidiary project. I can't sign every document personally, and it appears I was deliberately not informed about this proposal. Skiptree and her cronies were handling all the UK deals as subcontractors. As I've said, I've made sure heads will roll because of it. If I'd known, I'd have vetoed the whole idea. I really like your parents, and I'd never destroy all this."

Helen felt a sad smile forming and she gestured to the rust and cobwebs and general mess that was most definitely not in the style of the house of Almanza. "All this, you say? This tumbledown little old farm? I wish I could believe it was true, Ricardo, I really do."

"I'm not lying!"

Helen felt very weary. "So the fifty square miles. What are you going to do with all that? Are you planning on a constructing a new town or something? You could call it Almanzaville and surround Primrose Farm with skyscrapers if the planners let you. And they would let you, because you have plenty of money to grease the right palms."

"I heard this morning that I've secured permission to create a wildlife sanctuary with supporting infrastructure. No yachts, but a few canoes. No jets, but a lot of bird boxes. And places for children to play and families to spend time together. No casinos, nightclubs, or bars."

"Why?"

"Because I want us to stay as man and wife."

"But you don't believe in marriage."

"I didn't."

"So what's changed?"

"I've changed. You've made it happen, turned my world upside down and inside out and then kicked it in the balls." He thrust his hand underneath his armpits as if he was shivering with cold. "I thought I had my life all sorted, all tidied away in neat little boxes and then *you* happened. I've changed my mind. I think being married to you is wonderful and I don't want it to end. I want it to get better and better. I know it will. I want us to grow old together and be happy, be happy like your parents are."

Helen's head was beginning to spin, so much was happening. Her brain couldn't process it all. "You said you were bringing the divorce forward the last time we were together!"

"I was angry and hurt! You were shunning me, and my plans to ask you to marry me properly were all over the place. You were being impossible and I wasn't able to control the situation. I couldn't get you to do what I wanted you to without...telling you how I felt. I wasn't brave enough to risk everything, by opening myself up completely."

Helen heard a strange noise come out of her mouth, half whisper, half sob. She felt as if she was being sucked down a plughole, helpless, disorientated. Her world was at a tipping point. She could cling on, but she had to do the right thing. "I'm not pregnant, Ricardo. There's no baby, you don't have to say these things. You don't need to pretend. We can get divorced just like you'd always planned."

"Not pregnant?" His eyes seemed to grow darker against his paling skin. "I'm confused."

"No pregnancy, no baby, no need to be nice about this anymore."

"But why?"

"But why did my mum tell you I was?" She let out a sad laugh. "I'm not really sure. Wishful thinking, perhaps? Trying to get us back together the only way she could think of?"

"I see."

"I'm sorry you had to come all this way to hear the truth." She shrugged and watched herself push some damp hay around with the toe of her boot. "And that you got a good soaking in the process."

She saw his hand reach out to her from the corner of her eye and then she felt him gently grip her shoulder. "It doesn't matter," he whispered.

Holding back the tears was becoming painful. She needed to get away from him before she dissolved. "I'll go fetch you a dry towel and a hot drink before you go."

"It doesn't matter about the *baby*." His hand went to her chin and lifted her face to look at him. "It's you I want. A baby would be amazing, and I can't pretend I'm not disappointed, but I'd have come to fetch you soon anyway."

"Honestly?"

"I love you, Helen. That's what it all boils down to. I love you and I was too scared to say it in Spain, but now I have to if I stand any chance of getting you back, of persuading you to stay married to me. I don't want anything to come between us ever again." His voice grew hoarse as his hands dropped to his side and he took a step closer. "I want to help make your dreams come true."

Helen's head was spinning. "I don't know what to say."

Ricardo's breath was visible in the cold damp air, little clouds of hope and despair. "You left these behind," he said unfolding his long fingers to reveal two rings. "Will you put them on again? Will you be my wife? Properly this time? We can have a proper church blessing if you like with confetti, cameras, a thousand guests."

"You just said you loved me."

"I did. I do. I love you."

Helen's shoulders began to shake with emotion. "That's bloody amazing!"

"It's scaring the hell out of me."

"Why?"

His fingers closed around the rings and formed a tight fist. "Because I don't know how I'm going to make you love me back. I don't think even another million euros is going to make that happen. I'm scared I can never be enough for you."

She let out a ragged breath and grabbed the collar of his leather jacket. "Save your pennies, banker boy."

She'd never seen him look so completely shocked. His

voice was low and serious. "What do you mean?"

Helen touched her fingers to his mouth and pulled him closer. "I love you too, you rich sod." She took his empty hand, unfurled his fingers and then threaded them through hers. "And all I want is you and our future together. It's all I'll ever want."

Ricardo untangled their fingers and slid the rings back on to her left hand. "So it's official now. You're my wife to have and to hold forever."

"Do the lawyers need to draw up another addendum to cover this unusual and unexpected turn of events? Like how many sons I have to provide you with?"

He laughed and raindrops fell from his hair onto her nose. "No more bloody lawyers. Ever. And daughters will be fine."

"What if we can't…you know?"

"Then we'll have a lot of fun trying." He pulled her closer to him. "There's nothing wrong with just you and me, Helen. I'll do everything I can to make things perfect for you. Whatever you want, I'll try to give you, I promise."

Helen looked down at her left hand, still held in his and she believed him. "The rings are tighter than they were. All that gorgeous food and wine you stuffed me with in Spain. No wonder Mum convinced herself I was pregnant. I've come back at least half a stone heavier."

"And you look all the more gorgeous for it." He rubbed the back of his hand over her tummy and grinned. He brushed the water from her face and kissed her on the nose. "We'll have the rings altered. You can have a new set every year if you like. Or month or week, just so long as you say you'll stay my wife. I love you, and I can hardly dare to believe that this time it's for real."

"It always was real for me, the way I feel about you. I think I fell in love with you the first time I looked into your eyes and thought I was about to die. In a sort of way I did, because I'm in heaven now."

"Yes," he lowered his mouth to brush hers. "Amen to that."

Epilogue

"What a difference a year makes."

Helen snuggled into Ricardo as they leaned against an old apple tree in the farmyard. She loved being tucked under his arm and the feeling of protection it evoked. "Primrose Farm has changed so much—it looks clean, tidy, lucrative…"

Ricardo laughed. "Yes, thank God. This time last year I was doing a good impression of a drowned rat, remember? A muddy, miserable drowned rat."

"A bit like that lot over there." She nodded toward a group of bedraggled-looking individuals sipping hot punch on straw bales by a blazing fire pit. "Delegates from the latest corporate team-building course, Mum said. Bright young things all wanting to work in luxury yacht charter."

"That's one way of getting used to being damp all the time, I guess." He kissed her on the forehead and shuddered. "Rather them than me. They look shattered."

"So would you after two days living rough in the New Forest trying to prove your worth," she said with a chuckle. "They usually come back so cold and hungry. They eat anything put in front of them apparently."

"Signature steak pie and cabbage?"

"No! These companies pay so well that the residential courses are fully catered once they get back to base. There's a professionally staffed kitchen in the new barn conversion over there."

Ricardo looked over his shoulder to where she was pointing. "That decrepit barn. It's got a new roof."

"And proper windows. And two floors with bedrooms and a huge communal living area. Who'd have thought it was possible?" She could hardly believe how much the architectural transformation of the old building still thrilled her.

He smiled down at her mischievously. "Those contractors of mine did work hard pulling this place out of the muck, didn't they?"

"You paid them ludicrously well to get it all done in less than twelve months so we could go on holiday, you mean!"

"You were adamant about that as I recall, madam."

"I needed to see the new ventures up, running, and making a profit before I could enjoy myself. I needed closure on all the bad stuff that happened here. Needed to make sure Mum and Dad were looked after before starting my new life as Mrs. Almanza. I'm so grateful you understood that without me having to spell it out."

"I would have done exactly the same, and you've done a brilliant job of managing the project in the last year. You should be very proud." He squeezed her shoulder. "And now I have you all to myself again at last, but you do need to know that your mum's not very happy about where I'm taking you next week. I've had her on the phone again."

"You are joking?"

"No."

"I'll talk to her." She sighed. "Mum knows I've always

dreamed of going to Leptis Magna and Persepolis. They're two of the most amazing archaeological sites discovered in the last hundred years. I had pictures of them cut out from magazines all over my room as a teenager."

Ricardo shot her a wry look. "Unfortunately, she's just discovered they're located in Libya and Iran."

"I knew giving my parents a computer to play with was a mistake! Too much information. The pair of them are Google-mad these days." She smiled and looked down at her shoes for a moment. "This trip means so much to me. It's another dream about to come true. I can't thank you enough for everything you've done."

"You're my wife." He shrugged. "And it's only money."

"I know, but still."

"What I'd really like to see is your parents coming back from their long-awaited second honeymoon. The world's just waiting for them now there's an estate team running the events and farm shops. The money's pouring in. It's time they took it easy. They don't have to be slaves to the farm anymore."

"It'll happen, don't worry. Mum's raring to go, but Dad's finding it hard to hand over complete control, like someone else I know."

"Excuse me! This is the new Ricardo Almanza you're talking to here. The loving husband who's delegating all his business interests to scrabble around some ancient ruins with his bossy wife for six months."

"So you'll be leaving your smart phone and tablet behind?"

"That would be reckless." He jerked his chin upwards and stared into the middle distance. "I have your safety to consider, and communication with our security team must be maintained at all times. I promised your mother."

Helen elbowed him in the ribs and chuckled. "Conspiring behind my back again, eh? Cooking up deals with the She-Devil of homemade raspberry jam?"

"It's a simple strategy. You both get what you want and then it's my turn. In six months we start on my dreams." His expression became serious. "That's still the deal, right? You haven't changed your mind?"

"Are you mad? Of course not. I'm as excited about developing that old Spanish estate as you are. The vineyards, olive groves, almond and orange trees in the back garden and…"

"And?"

Helen felt herself blush as his golden eyes burned into her. Ricardo still had the ability to make her heart rate triple with just one look. Her voice dropped to a whisper. "And then starting a family."

He brushed a strand of hair away from her smiling face. She seemed to grow more beautiful by the day, and in that brief moment he felt more vulnerable than he ever had. "I love you, Mrs. Almanza, do you know that?"

"Do I get that in writing?"

"Seriously, it's so real it hurts." He lifted her left hand to his lips and kissed the tip of her ring finger. "Don't ever leave me, Helen."

"As if. I love you too and you know it." Her eyes glittered with unshed tears. "Besides, it's too late. The deal's been made, so you're stuck with me now."

He threaded his fingers through hers and gripped her hand tightly. "For better or for worse?"

"For *good*."

Acknowledgments

Thanks go to …

Colin for being my rock, tolerating my obsessions and pairing up the socks.

Rebecca for teaching herself to cook, making sure I shut the front door and being so beautiful.

Joseph for not minding when I forget things, making me laugh and jumping in puddles.

The fabulous team at Entangled publishing, producing wonderful books and very happy authors. You guys work so hard.

About the Author

Rachel writes full-time when her children are at school, but is still proud of her law degree and accountancy qualifications. She has worked in the space industry, pharmaceuticals, insurance, a supermarket, a bus station, a railway depot, and a lingerie department. She lives with her daughter, son, and The Exec in Fareham, Hampshire, on the south coast of England and can sometimes smell the sea from her back garden. When not working, her hobbies include rummaging through antique shops, talking to her chocolate brown Rex rabbit and popping into Sainsbury's. She also has a fondness for wine and expensive lipstick. Rachel loves to hear from readers. Visit her at http://rachellyndhurst.blogspot.com.